The Road to Summering

Maureen Pople began writing in 1976, and has since won numerous prizes, including the National Short Story of the Year Award and the Henry Lawson Award for Prose. She is the author of *The Other Side of the Family* (1986) and *Pelican Creek* (1989), and in 1989 was awarded a Writer's Fellowship by the Literature Board of the Australia Council.

The Road to Summering

MAUREEN POPLE

University of Queensland Press

First published 1990 by University of Queensland Press
Box 42, St Lucia, Queensland 4067 Australia

© Maureen Pople 1990

This book is copyright. Apart from any fair dealing
for the purposes of private study, research, criticism
or review, as permitted under the Copyright Act, no
part may be reproduced by any process without written
permission. Enquiries should be made to the publisher.

Typeset by University of Queensland Press
Printed in Australia by The Book Printer, Melbourne

Distributed in the USA and Canada by
International Specialized Book Services, Inc.,
5602 N.E. Hassalo Street, Portland, Oregon 97213-3640

Creative writing program assisted
by the Literature Board of the
Australia Council, the Federal Government's
arts funding and advisory body

Cataloguing in Publication Data

National Library of Australia

Pople, Maureen, 1928- .
  The road to Summering.

  I. Title.

A823.3

ISBN 0 7022 2267 4

FOR JOHN

1

Rachel walked into the kitchen of her father's house. There was the customary pile of unwashed dishes by the sink, and more on the table. She looked around the room. *You could eat off this floor, a solid three course meal — it's all there — but if they think I'm going to offer to clean up this time they can think again.*

"Anyone home?" she called. "It's me."

Her father's bass and Caroline's contralto warbled a short, welcoming duet from the front of the house and her father added his habitual coda. "Make us a cup of coffee will you, love?"

Now why don't I go straight to the kettle and brew up the minute I come to this place? I swear if I came bursting in here one day screaming that a maniac with a gun was after me, he'd say, "Coming. And make us a cup of coffee will you, love?"

She put the kettle on and began the usual fruitless search for clean cups, and as usual gave up, selected a pile of the more recently used china and began washing.

Thing is, what would he deal with first? Maniac or coffee? Well, we know the answer to that one, don't we?

Caroline padded into the room. Her feet were bare and

rather grubby, and she was wearing an extremely dirty man's shirt over an only slightly less dirty pair of jeans. Her hair had been hauled up and fixed in a chignon, but only a few strands were still up there; most of it was hanging around her neck in a cluster of greying curls. She was covered in mud up to her armpits and her face was streaked with what appeared at first to be chocolate, but which, no doubt, was mud as well. So in fact her feet were the cleanest part of her.

"Hello. Shan't kiss you." Rachel was mightily relieved. Apart from resenting the familiarity, if she wanted mud she was prepared to collect her own, not take it secondhand. "You don't mean to tell me there's no washing-up been done?"

Well I wasn't going to bother, but since you bring the matter up, there's no washing-up been done. Not since the last time I was here I imagine.

"Pa wanted coffee, and there aren't any clean cups."

"You do sound tired. Was it a strain, pedalling all the way out here?"

"Bit. But I'm all right now, thanks." *If you really want to know the main strain was persuading Ma to let me come. As usual.*

"Look, you go inside and chat to Himself. I'll do this. Go on, I'll wash all of these and make the coffee and bring you in a nice hot cup in half a jiffy." She waved her muddy paws at the dishes. Rachel cut her off, putting her arms around the sink and her dear clean suds. "Oh, yes," Caroline murmured, "I suppose I should clean up first. Back in a moment." And she wandered from the room.

Rachel continued to chip at the bonded grime. Their acquaintance was short, but she knew that Caroline would forget what she had planned to do the minute something new caught her eye, and washing-up seemed to be well down on her list of interests. The water boiled, she poured it on to the coffee grounds and finished her quota of dishes while it infused. Then she loaded a tray with clean mugs and the coffee-maker and carried it up the hallway to the sitting room at the front of the house.

"Coffee's up." She kneed magazines, books, and newspapers on to the floor from the coffee table and set the tray down, then evicted even more of the same from the sofa to make a space to sit.

Caroline came in wearing fresh, but unpressed, shirt and jeans. Her face and hands were scrubbed, except for her fingernails which were broken off short and each weighed down with a load of dried clay. She grabbed at her hair and hauled the rebel strands back and up but missed the comb so that most of them fell down again immediately.

She's completely forgotten that washing-up. What on earth does he see in her? What got into him? She arrives in town and within two days he leaves a perfectly good wife and family and races her off out here. I've got to face the fact I guess, my father is completely mad!

Her father walked in at that moment, grabbed Caroline, and gave her such a hug and kissed her so thoroughly on the neck, that her hair gave up the struggle completely and all tumbled down. She didn't seem to mind, but tilted her head slightly in Rachel's direction and he then came over and gave his daughter a similar greeting.

"How's my girl?" He held her away from him and examined her face carefully. "How's my baby girl?" Suddenly his grotty old kitchen ceased to offend her and she rubbed her cheek against his beard as she used to do when times were happier and problems not so pressing.

"Okay thanks, Pa," she said. "How's the book coming along?"

"Listen, kid," he growled, "first law of good behaviour. Never ask a writer how his book's coming along. Books never 'come along', they are cranked out with an inordinate amount of effort and agony by a poor benighted writer, who'd be much better off financially and physically if he spent his time washing the dishes in a chophouse."

"Sorry I asked."

"As the old Somerset Maugham himself once said, 'There are three rules for writing the novel. Unfortunately no one knows what they are.' He was right."

"Not going well, huh?"

"Not too badly, actually. Things are steaming up reasonably well."

I'm steaming up reasonably well too, actually.

"And your mother?"

"She's worried sick if you really want to know. About B's new boyfriend."

She saw them look at each other, a look she couldn't fathom, but it seemed to have a deep meaning to them. Her father sighed, and took a noisy slurp of coffee.

"Darling girl, your mother studies worry as a doctor studies medicine, a priest theology. To less purpose of course, but with just as much dedication. What does she claim is *wrong* with B's new boyfriend? No. I think I'll pass on this one. Make up my own mind when I meet him."

Oh no you don't. This is your daughter we're talking about here. Start making your mind up now. Please, Pa.

"Name's Joe, sort of," she said, careful to keep her tone calm and free of all critical nuances. "He's quite nice really."

"Nice! Quite nice! Quite nice really! Well, that tells us *quite* a lot, doesn't it, Caroline?"

Caroline giggled into her coffee mug. "Stop teasing her, Mac," she snorted.

"And what do you mean by 'sort of', eh? Either the boy's name's Joe or it isn't. How can it be Joe, sort of?

Unless he's . . ." he hit his forehead as if a mighty piece of knowledge had just struck him. "Of course. I see now why your mother's worried. The lad's Russian. Our eldest child has taken up with a Bolshevik. A Commie. Joe Sortof. Does he wear one of those fur hats and is there snow on his boots?".

"Oh do be quiet, Mac. I'm hungry. Come on, Rachel, help me find some food, eh?"

Rachel stepped over her father's outstretched feet and glared at him as she did. So he opened his eyes wide in a look of hurt innocence. His "Who me?" look. She went back and gave him a swift kick in the shin, regretting deeply that she was wearing joggers that wouldn't hurt him much, but he howled in a satisfactory manner *then* she followed Caroline to the kitchen.

They found some wilted lettuce and celery in the crisper of the refrigerator and Caroline ran it under cold water and talked to it sternly until it perked up and was persuaded to be almost crisp again. There was a jar of black olives that needed only to be rinsed to get the mould off, and two tomatoes that tasted quite fresh when the bad bits were excised. She put it all into a big pottery bowl, then opened a tin of tuna and tossed it in with French dressing while Rachel found a battered wooden tray and loaded it with plates and cutlery from her recent washing-up, a length of brightly coloured batik for a tablecloth, pottery goblets and a cask of cheap white wine.

They set the meal up on the old redwood table under the big gum tree in the back yard, and Caroline with a flourish brought out a fresh loaf she'd baked that morning. Rachel was slightly miffed that it smelled and tasted so good. Like her mother, she believed that bread-making should be left to the baker, and that people who baked their own were odd and inclined to be show-offs. Better if she spent a bit more time cleaning up this dump and a bit less time baking fancy bread, she thought as she munched on her third slice.

Her father squirted soda from the old-fashioned syphon into her wine and his own, then took a long sip as if to give himself strength. "And how's young George these days?" he said.

Rachel wondered why the question, which he asked each time, was always so difficult to answer without embarrassment.

"He's all right, Pa. I dropped him at the pictures on the way out here. There's a Humphrey Bogart festival on. It's *Casablanca*. He's been looking forward to . . ."

"I know, duck, don't worry about it. Young George will come round in his own good time. Now tell me. What is it you don't like about your sister's young man. Eh?"

"Nothing," Rachel protested, helping herself to more salad, "I've only met him a couple of times. He's great. Ma thinks she's a bit young, that's all. B's really serious this time and she is only twenty. No, I like Joe. I like him very much. Very much indeed."

Her father grinned. "The lady doth protest too much, methinks," he murmured. "Never mind, love, after a few years it'll hardly hurt at all."

Rachel sucked on an olive pip and decided that her father was indeed completely mad.

2

Janet Huntley was pushing the veranda chairs into one straight row when Rachel and George arrived home.

"Don't walk on the kitchen floor, I've just washed it," she called.

Hello to you too.

Rachel tipped George off the bar and handed him the bike to put away.

"Hi, Ma."

"How is your father?"

Now here was a problem. No matter how she answered this question she knew that all the muscles of her mother's face would tighten up immediately and that a chilly breeze would begin to blow. So she spoke very quickly, groping meanwhile for a change of subject.

"Okay. He's okay. The book's coming along. Steaming up, I think he said. Beatrice home yet?"

Sure enough all the muscles of her mother's face tightened up immediately and a chilly breeze began to blow. "And her? What about her? Still spinning those horseruggy skirts of hers?"

George cravenly slid away towards the back of the house.

"She wove them, the skirts, it was the wool she spun." *Oh hell, how do I get into these messes?* "It's pottery now. He bought her a kiln for her birthday." *Whoops, that was a mistake. Why don't I learn to keep my mouth shut?*

"Oh well. Of course he would, wouldn't he? *I* went without the bare necessities of life, to say nothing of any luxuries, for years when you were young, and now he buys HER kilns."

"It's only the one kiln, Ma." Rachel looked around her at the comfortable house and well-kept garden, trying to remember a time when the bare necessities of life had been missing. "B home yet?"

But Beatrice wasn't home. For the third time that week she was out with the new boyfriend. So Rachel spent a dreary evening watching television and wondering what those two could possibly think of to talk about for so long. Her mother sat in the big chair carefully unpicking a cardigan she'd knitted two years previously for her husband, in the days before he ran off with "her".

If my husband left me for another woman the very last thing I'd want to do would be to unpick his old cardigan to make up again. Or is it just one of your waste not want nots?

"Waste not want not," her mother said, reading Rachel's mind in the uncanny way she sometimes had. "This is imported wool; it's French, and I've always loved this green. It's a pity not to see it worn by someone."

"I'll take it and give it back to Pa next time I go if you like."

"If you two're going to keep yakking I'm going to bed, listen to the radio. Nothing on the box anyway. S'long." George hurried bedwards with a short detour to the kitchen to gather supplies to see him through the night.

"Hates talking about Pa, doesn't he? But really, Ma,

you always said it looked great on him. Why don't you give it back?"

Her mother clutched the bundle of disjointed arms, backs and side fronts and stuffed them down behind her on the chair, and Rachel marvelled that the gesture seemed so fond and protective. And sad. After all, it was only a bundle of wool.

"You know, Ma, that colour suits you! Why don't you make it up into one of those big sweaters with a shawl neck and incredibly long? It brings up your eyes, honestly."

Mrs Huntley dragged the bundle out from behind her, "You really think so? I did wonder about something for me. I don't suppose you or Beatrice . . ."

"No. Suits you best, and it's a shame to waste it."

Her mother, smiling like a young girl just engaged, began to unpick again.

Love! Yuk! If ever I fall in love so help me I'll kill myself.

She was pondering ways of doing that without ending up too bloody or indecent when a truck pulled up outside the house. She waited for five minutes, then waking her mother from what seemed to be a pleasant daydream she said, "She's home. I heard them ages ago. I'll just wander out. Say hello."

"You'll do no such thing!" Her mother lifted her head so that she could see through the window. "They're parked right under the street light anyway."

Oh well, in that case everything's fine. Bet if I stayed out there with a boy for five seconds, street light or not, you'd be yelling at me to come inside. "Oh well, in that case everything's fine."

"Don't be insolent, Rachel, and isn't it time for bed? I'll be glad when you're back at school, you're so restless these days. I wonder if it's wise for you to visit your father and that woman so often."

"Ma! It's only once a fortnight! You agreed!"

"Yes, I did agree. But I still can't understand why you want to go all the way out there . . ."

"I'm curious, that's all. Honestly, Ma. Want to find out what she's like. You know. And what do you mean I'm restless? I'm not restless, just bored, and that reminds me. All right if I see about getting a job for the rest of the holidays?"

"He should never have stayed here. Once he decided to go off with her they should have had the decency to move somewhere else."

"They could hardly move away, Ma. She's got the Craft Centre and he's got the shop."

"Well, I don't know how they can face people in town after what they did to us."

"Facing people's never been a problem for Pa. I don't think he really knows other people are around, unless it's someone he's specially fond of. Beatrice and Joe sure must have a lot to talk about. They've been parked out there for hours."

A door slammed outside, then another one, and two pairs of footsteps came up the path.

Now it'll take another half an hour for them to finally say good night! "Think I should open the door? Maybe she's lost her key."

Her mother, still happily unravelling the cardigan, smiled. "Why don't you switch off that television if you're not watching it. She'll be here in a minute, we can all go to bed then."

"Ma, why did you stay on? I mean when Pa and Caroline took off together, why didn't you want to go away? I would have, I think."

Her mother took a long time untying a knot in the wool, so long that Rachel wondered if she planned to answer the question at all.

"Of course I wanted to go away," she said finally. "I was humiliated and embarrassed. Still am. It was almost impossible to walk up the street — still is — because I knew that everyone in town knew about the affair. And it happened so suddenly! But with Beatrice halfway through her course, and you and George at school what can I do? I have to stay."

I wouldn't, I'll tell you that right now.

"It's over three and a half months since they moved out there. It doesn't get any easier for me, but I'll manage. What's their house like?"

You ask that every time.

"Oh, you know, just a farmhouse. Nothing special."

"Good housekeeper is she? Your father always likes things to be neat and tidy."

Oh yeah? Not any more he doesn't.

"Well I guess things aren't as well organised as they were here. I mean now that he doesn't go to the store any more and he's busy writing the book. You know."

"He still couldn't bear an untidy house!"

"Untidy? Oh no, I wouldn't call it untidy. It's okay, Ma."

What would I call it? Slovenly? Chaotic? The grottiest mess I've ever seen, that's probably what I'd call it. But not to you, Ma. Thanks all the same!

"Well I'm glad of that. I don't want your father to be uncomfortable, no matter what he and Caroline Summers have done to me. Here's Beatrice now. Hello, dear. Did you have a pleasant evening?"

Beatrice floated into the room. Rachel quickly shoved her bare and unwashed feet under the coffee table. Beatrice eased the jacket from her shoulders and shook her long fair hair. Rachel squirmed her fingers through her short brown shag and longed for blondeness and sophistication.

"Hey, everyone, listen," Beatrice murmured in a soft and breathy voice, "guess what. Joe's asked me to marry him, and I said I would. Oh Ma, oh Rach, isn't it wonderful?"

Mrs Huntley stood up with the suddenness and speed of a jack-in-the-box, scattering pieces of knitting in every direction.

"Oh! Darling! No!"

Well, that's a pretty direct answer, I must say!

"Aren't you pleased, Ma?"

"Well . . . it's a shock, that's all." Her mother took a long deep breath, put out her arms and hugged Beatrice, then kissed her gently on the cheek. "Of course I'm pleased for you, dear, it's just that we hardly know your young man yet, do we? It seems that you're so young. Do you have to rush into it so quickly?"

Mother! A little tact here, please!

But dear old Beatrice kept smiling her goofy smile and stood back the more easily to look her mother in the eye.

"We just want to be married soon, that's all."

"Darling! Well that's wonderful news. Fancy, only twenty years old and going to be married. That is wonderful news, isn't it Rachel?" But she sounded unconvinced.

"Yeah. Great B. That's great."

Yeah. T'rific.

3

The main street was wide enough to take a row of cars parked rear to kerb on each side, an intermittent passage of vehicles up and down the middle, and Rachel Huntley pedalling her bicycle languidly between the two.

She pulled in between a small truck laden with large bales of fencing wire and a dusty Volvo station wagon with two blue cattle dogs having a serious discussion together behind the back seat. One of them leaned out through the window and gave her a damp nudge as she propped the bike against the kerb. She tickled his ear for a moment, then of course had to do the same for his friend and would have stayed there for ever if the dogs had had their way.

She left them finally and entered the bank. The manager saw her over the glass partition of his office and hurried out to welcome her. His interest declined when he found that she'd come to ask for employment and not to augment her account, but he kindly suggested that she should come back when she finished school, *then* he would be happy to take her on permanently. He managed to give the impression that to have such a valued old customer on his staff he would be prepared to dismiss anyone she chose and offer the vacant job to her.

She left her bike where it was to avoid another session with the over-friendly dogs, and walked along the footpath. Barry's Butchery was next to the bank but she decided not to try for a job there. There just might be one, and the thought of working among all those vast and bloody carcases rather put her off.

Then there was her father's shop, taking up the rest of the block. MACINTOSH B. HUNTLEY & SON, GENERAL STORE was painted along the front above the windows. The paint was fading and flaking on the letters, although the rest of the building was neat and well preserved, and Rachel knew why. Her father hated his name.

The original Macintosh B. had been a mean and moody old great-grandfather who founded the store and insisted that his eldest son take it over. That son had likewise insisted and so had his son. So, Macintosh Bs all of them, they had kept up the good old family tradition, bullied their offspring, and renewed the paint on the sign regularly.

Until the current Macintosh B. came along. Not only did he have his boy child christened George (not even George B., just George), but also he allowed the sign to go unpainted year after year, hoping no doubt that it would finally fade away completely. To further affront the ghosts of his forefathers he installed computers in the office of the store. And while they were still spinning, scandalised, in their respective graves, he *really* kicked over the traces. He stopped working in the store entirely (they spun faster). He left his wife of twenty-two years and his three children, and went off to live in an old farmhouse with the woman who had come to open the Craft Centre. Just two days after she arrived in town. And he began to write The Great Australian Novel. If it had been possible, no doubt every Macintosh B. in the cemetery would have died again from the shock of it all.

Rachel hurried past. The entire staff had known her all her life; most of them were old enough to have known her father all *his* life, and she doubted if a single one of them approved of what he had done. But she suspected that for them his greatest sin was not running off with Caroline, but giving up working in the store. To each of them it was a vocation rather than a job and whenever she entered the place she felt them smiling at her, with infinite pity and kindness, seeming to silently deplore the fact that she had a father who'd lost his wits. The knowledge that she was inclined to agree with them didn't help her either.

She crossed the road to the Royal Hotel and grinned at the expression that would lay waste her mother's face if she were to announce that she'd found employment at the Royal! On the other hand a pharmacy would be just right, she decided, so she breezed into Mr Walker's chemist shop. A girl she knew only as Sandra wiggled out from behind the cosmetics counter, hobbled by the tightness and shortness of her white uniform. She flapped dense eyelashes and patted snow-white hair.

"Help you?" she whispered. "Wachel innit?"

Rachel stood dumb, poleaxed, completely unstrung by envy and admiration. She allowed herself to ponder for a moment on the joys of working with wise and brilliant Sandra, of getting in there among the stocks of make-up, scents and hair-dyes.

"Hello, Sandra," she finally managed to croak. "Haven't seen you since you left school. You look great. Mr Walker in?"

"Yeth. He'th in." She offered no more, but stood, her face immobile, her hands moving all the time, smoothing her skirt, her hair, each other, with caressing strokes as if she had made it all herself and was afraid that some of it, if neglected for a moment, might begin to crack and fall apart.

"Well, may I speak to him for a minute, please?"
Those eyelashes! They're purple! Wow!
"Yeth. He'th up the back." Sandra's head moved ever so slightly to show Rachel where the back of the shop and the owner could be found, but her hypnotic hazel eyes never closed and her lips hung slightly open after she spoke.

You close those eyes just once baby and they stick together forever I guess. Wow! And your lipstick goes right up inside to your gums. How do you do *that?*

"Thanks, Sandra. You look great. Did I already say that? Well you do. Thanks." She backed away from Sandra who was now teetering slightly, able to stand for only so long on her astonishingly long legs and her steeple-high heels.

Mr Walker was no help. "Hey, Rachel darling, if I had work for him I'd get that shiftless great son of mine in here, pay him special family rates you understand? A pittance. But no, nothing doing. Young Sandra's pretty efficient you know."

Young Sandra had retreated behind the counter and was leaning against it resting her feet and carefully filing a nail with a long emery board. She wasn't *looking* particularly efficient, but no doubt she was capable of leaping into action should the need arise. "She's certainly stunning to look at, Mr Walker," Rachel admitted.

Mr Walker stared at his young assistant as if he'd never seen her before. "You think so?" he said. "Couple of people have mentioned that. Don't see it myself, but she's a good little worker."

Rachel remembered that Mrs Walker was small and round and bouncy and that whenever they were together she and Mr Walker walked hand-in-hand and looked at each other when they spoke, so she guessed that the chemist really did see only a good little worker in the gorgeous and glamorous Sandra.

"Anyway, only get two weeks holiday don't you? No use getting a job for that length of time surely? That's what my lad tells me anyway. Mind you he is quite exceptionally lazy, that boy." He smiled, proud of having such a gifted son.

"S'pose so. It's not really long enough to dig in, is it? I probably shan't bother. Thanks anyway." She walked out, slowing down as she passed Sandra who nodded serenely at her and wiggled three red-crested fingernails.

Wow, I bet I could look as good as that if I could just find me a job. It is unfair!

"'Bye, Sandra, 'bye, Mr Walker."

Outside on the footpath she came face to face with Caroline Summers. This was a considerably cleaned-up version of the weekend woman. Now she was wearing well-cut black pants, and a cream silk shirt with a red-and-cream spotted cravat at the neck, the same red-and-cream spotted cravat that Rachel remembered her father getting as a present for his birthday some years before. From herself. The tweed jacket she was wearing had a familiar look to it as well, but the big leather shoulder-bag was her own, obviously a product of the Craft Centre, and her hair was demure in a bun at the back of her neck.

"Hi," she said, "want a cup of coffee? I'm heading back to the Centre, why don't you collect your bike and come along? Ride fast and you might just beat me to it."

Oh sure, we can't be seen walking together, can we? And we can't go into the coffee shop and sit down like civilised people and have coffee together, can we? People might talk, mightn't they?

"I thought I was only supposed to see you once a fortnight."

"I think that just means your father. Well, good

heavens, child, we can hardly avoid seeing each other in the street sometimes. Don't worry so much about what other people think, come if you want to, don't come if you'd rather not. Simple. I shan't be offended."

It's not quite as clear-cut as that, Caroline, and you know it isn't.

"Well, actually I don't think I will this time, thanks. I'm looking for a job you see. Not having much luck so far, well no luck at all to be honest, and I'm wondering if it's worth it, we only get two weeks off anyway."

"Well you must decide, darling. Look, if you're a bit short of cash your Pa and I could . . ."

Oh wow! And I can just hear Ma. Where'd you get the money, Rachel? And me saying from Pa and Caroline, Mummy dear. And then my bones being scattered all over the place, without the benefit of anaesthetic too. No, thank you, I couldn't stand the pain.

"No thank you, Caroline, really, I'm fine. It's more for something to do than the money."

That's not true, of course. The money is the main thing and I'd certainly like to get started on some of that stuff Sandra uses.

"Look, seriously darling, we could always do with another pair of hands at the Centre. Why not ask your mother and if she doesn't mind . . ."

Caroline! You don't know *my mother!*

"Not much of a job, making coffee for customers, tidying up, that sort of thing, but we'd love to have you. Think about it anyway and phone me. We'd pay enough to keep the wolf from the door. Well, a small wolf, anyway. Say a cub. Say a puny, undernourished cub?" she grinned. "So phone me, right?"

And away she went, leaving Rachel standing, miserable, on the footpath. Two women went by and stopped talking as they did so; she could feel them looking at her and the departing Caroline with sly interest so she used some advice her father had given her when he was leaving them.

"Look 'em straight in the eye, Rachel, when they don't expect you to. It's a very disconcerting trick, and one you may need to use from time to time."

She turned suddenly; both women were looking over their shoulders at her. She looked them in the eye, one after the other, and embarrassed they turned away.

It works, Pa, I guess they were disconcerted all right, but it certainly doesn't make me feel any better.

She collected her bicycle, noting that the friendly dogs had gone, then she rode slowly home.

4

"It's because I didn't let you go on that camp, isn't it? That's why you've been so difficult these holidays."

"No it's not, Ma. I didn't want to go to the stupid camp. Who wants to go all the way to the Snowy Mountains to look at plants anyway?"

And learn to ski, and stay at a ritzy motel? Me for one!

"Well I'm sorry, Rachel, but I'm not going to change my mind about this. Top right-hand corner. No, no, that's the left, I said right. Top right. There, put some more spray on it before you rub."

"It's too late to change your mind anyway, they left at the weekend, and what do you mean, 'difficult'?"

Oh cancel that question, please! Here I am, marooned up a ladder cleaning windows and I start an argument that won't stop for three days. At least.

But her mother was too intent on cleaning the house, and not in a mood to quarrel with her assistant, so the question was, in fact, cancelled in favour of more important matters.

"Never mind, dear. You can start on the next one now, shall I move the ladder?"

"Not with me on it again please! Look, Ma, how about I

20

finish the windows, AND move the ladder, and you can go inside and tidy up there."

"Tidy up! It's more than a tidy up I'll have you know, Rachel. I'll need you to help me beat the rugs when you've done the windows — better launder the bedroom curtains right away — then there's all the silver to be cleaned."

She bustled off around the side of the house, still busy cataloguing jobs to be done, and Rachel leaned on a rung of the ladder and gazed bleakly after her.

A few people to dinner you said, Ma. It's not as if the whole entire line-up of the Royals is coming to inspect the place. Blimey, those lucky pigs at the snow.

George wobbled home on his bicycle looking for lunch and was immediately coralled in the kitchen at a table laden with the family silver, a pile of old singlets and torn-up pyjamas and a large bottle of silver polish. His mother promised him a tuna sandwich later, and Rachel, hoping to keep him on the job and reasonably content to stay there, smuggled him the earphones for the radio so that he could listen to whatever he wanted, as loud as he wanted. George was grateful, but he glared moodily about him as he rubbed the forks and fruitbowls, looking like a caged and hungry tiger. Rachel retreated to the back yard to help her mother beat the Persian rugs.

Each rug was hung over the clothes line and they began by standing one each side of it to bash with their lengths of broom-handle. When each of them was choking with dust they realised that something was wrong with their technique, so Rachel moved around to stand beside her mother and they belted together until no more dust came out. Rachel enjoyed walloping the rugs, and decided that it was the one household chore she wouldn't mind doing on a permanent basis. It was a very satisfying job.

While the three of them ate their sandwich luncheon on the outside table so that George's silver cleaning would not be disturbed (his mother's idea, definitely not George's), Rachel decided that this would be as good a time as any to find out what the cleaning binge was all about. She had been wakened early that morning and presented with a choice of jobs. Not a choice of which she would do, but a choice of which order she would choose to do them in. Her mother had been in one of her "don't bother me now, dear, I'm busy", moods, offering only the fact that a dinner was involved, but she seemed calmer now, so Rachel waded in, finding the water deeper than she had expected.

"Now you're asking some people for dinner, right? Who?"

"Whom, Rachel, I think that should be *whom*. Well Joseph, of course . . ."

George, with a mouthful of tuna sandwich, found it difficult to catch his breath. "Joseph?" he finally spluttered, "Joseph? His name's not Joseph is it? She told me Joe, Beatrice said Joe. Joseph, hey, I can't stand it! Tell me it's not true!"

Rachel giggled with him. "Calls himself Joe. More likely to be Guiseppe I suppose. Guiseppe Deladro."

"Beatrice Deladro." Her mother balanced the names. "It doesn't sound *too* bad, does it? Quite aristocratic. I wonder what the family does, back in Italy. I must remember to ask his mother. I'm inviting her too of course, his mother, a sort of family party to celebrate the engagement. I thought Saturday night. We should have the house finished by then."

It and me too.

"What about Pa?"

"I thought I'd do a buffet. Or do you think a roast?"

"If it's a family party you'll have to invite Pa, and . . ."

George stuffed the rest of his sandwich into his mouth and stood up. "I'll get back to the silver then."

Mrs Huntley reached out and grabbed his arm. "Wait a moment, George," she said, and her voice was high and fast. "I suppose we'll have to talk about this."

"*You* two talk about it. Nothing to do with me. I'm going to the pictures Saturday anyway."

"Doesn't matter, Ma." Suddenly Rachel felt that she too would rather not take part in the discussion that seemed to be looming. But her mother pushed George back into his chair, plonked her elbows down among the plates and glasses and began to speak, looking sternly at a shred of lettuce that was lying in a soggy pool on the tablecloth.

"Beatrice, your sister, as you know, has agreed to marry Joseph."

Blimey!

"Now it is customary, on occasions such as this, that the parents of the bride, despite any misgivings they may have about the union, invite the family of the groom to some sort of gathering, to meet, and get to know each other, because, of course, they will be members of the family after the wedding. Do you understand that, George?"

George, longing to be somewhere else, nodded impatiently, but with a look that clearly showed that he had not, in fact, understood a word of it.

"I say the parents of the bride, but in this case, since your father has chosen to desert his family and go to live with that woman, the task will devolve upon me."

Devolve!

"But you could ask them to come too, Ma."

"Them! Ask *them!* I hardly think that my duties as mother of the bride-to-be include inviting your father's, your father's, friend, to join us at dinner, Rachel, after all it *is* a family occasion."

"Right. I reckon they don't have to come. Just us and

Joe and his mum and that's enough. If that's all that's coming do I have to clean *all* that silver stuff then, Ma?"

Mrs Huntley examined that lettuce as if it were a germ under her microscope. "Yes, George, I'm afraid it all has to be done. And of course Rachel is right. I do have to invite your father along. Beatrice is his daughter too, she'll want him I suppose. I must not be small-minded about this. I shall do the right thing, no matter what it costs me."

Hoping to bring the cosy conversation to an end for all of their sakes, Rachel said, "I think a buffet sounds like hard work, Ma. Why not do a roast, easier for you."

"Whatever I do won't be easy, I can assure you, Rachel. We'll have a buffet, and you will be here George, no movie that night. I'll telephone them all this evening. Now let's get on with this cleaning or the house will never be ready."

So they got on with it, Rachel wondering when it would be tactful to broach the subject of working at Caroline's Craft Centre. Probably never, she decided, and certainly not today when her mother was tearing about the house like a demented skivvy, scrubbing, polishing or scouring everything that would hold still long enough for her to set upon it.

Beatrice arrived home just as they were all about to fall over from exhaustion. Well, Mrs Huntley still appeared to have some steam up, but Rachel and George were crotchety and glassy-eyed. She drifted in and typically failed to notice that the house was bright with cleanliness, that the windows glinted, the silver gleamed and the glassware glistened.

"Not seeing Joe tonight. He's working on an assignment," she said. "So why don't we all go out to the movies or something?"

Even George turned the invitation down.

She listened to the plans for the dinner party, and agreed with her mother that a buffet would be best, but just as

Mrs Huntley was about to telephone the Deladros to invite them, she dropped her bombshell.

"She won't come, of course. Joe's mother. She won't come."

"Of course she will darling, that's the whole idea, to give the families a chance to get to know each other. I'm even going to ask your father. Of course she'll come."

"She won't you know. Doesn't want us to get married at all." Beatrice's lovely face slumped into sad lines, but only for a moment, then she brightened up. "But Joe would love to come and really get to know the family."

George brightened too, "Great," he said, "let's just have Joe and then you don't have to bother about asking Pa. That'll be great."

"George, you may go and watch television. I'll call you when dinner is ready. Rachel, please excuse us, your sister and I have some things to talk about."

Wow! Look out B.

She and George speedily left the room, George thankfully and Rachel with some reluctance at missing out on the topics that her mother and Beatrice would be covering. She felt she might be of some help there, but there was no welcome on her mother's face, so she went to the kitchen and warmed up last night's steak-and-kidney leftovers. She loitered hopefully by the door, but heard nothing, because George had abandoned the headphones and had the television on full-bore.

When Beatrice and her mother finally came out of the front room they were both showing signs of wear and tear. George and Rachel were the only ones who had any appetite for dinner; poor, pale Beatrice retired early to bed and Mrs Huntley took up her position by the telephone and resolutely began to dial.

5

The next day had to be lived through to be believed. Rachel had lain awake for a long time, listening to the faint murmur of her mother's voice and praying devoutly that all the invitees might have unbreakable appointments for every evening of the next five years.

At breakfast, however, they were forced once more into an acknowledgment of family obligations.

"I spoke to Mrs Deladro last night. Her English is certainly not as good as I'd expected, Beatrice. In fact it's very sketchy indeed."

Oh come on, Ma. I bet your Italian isn't too crash hot come to that.

"She manages." Beatrice spoke up defensively. "She's a very, ah, nice woman, when you get to know her."

"Yes. I'm sure she is." Her mother let the silence run on a trifle too long and Rachel cringed. It seemed that Mrs Deladro had somehow failed the test. More than one test actually, since Beatrice's opinion was somewhat lukewarm as well.

George had noticed the coolness too, and stopped crunching toast just long enough to mutter, "So wassa matta widda poor old broad?"

"I don't think all those gangster films are doing you any good, George. There is nothing at all the matter with the poor old broa . . . with Mrs Deladro. She was reluctant at first to come to dinner here, I imagine she might feel a little self-conscious, out of place, but I managed to convince her that Joe would want her to come, and she agreed. I think. It's very difficult to understand what she's saying. But you must all help to make her feel comfortable now. Her background may not be the same as ours, but we're simple people, not pretentious, and it's our, well our duty, no it's our privilege, to make her feel at home here."

Well I just hope poor illiterate old Mrs Deladro realises how gracious and condescending we all are! Honestly, Ma, what gets into you!

"If she really isn't keen to come, wouldn't it make her feel more comfortable if we let the whole thing drop? I mean then she could *stay* at home, as well as feeling at home."

George beamed and wiggled a thumb in approval, Beatrice pushed some muesli around her plate and moaned, "I told you, Ma, she really doesn't want to come. Doesn't want Joe and me to be married. I agree with Rach, let's drop it."

But Mrs Huntley, having succeeded so far, was determined to persevere. "I also telephoned your father. Trouble there, I'm afraid. I did think that I had made my position clear. I asked *him* to come to dinner on Saturday evening. He agreed to come. I told him it was to meet Joe and to celebrate your engagement, Beatrice, and he agreed that we should do that. Then, just as I was about to hang up he said he must check whether that woman was free on Saturday evening. He came back to the phone and said that she was. Now I made it perfectly clear that she was not invited, I had stressed that he was to come alone and yet he had the effrontery to presume that I had included her."

Rachel took care not to look in George's direction. She could hear his strangled giggles, which, combined with the slurps he always made eating toast were producing some pretty disgusting noises altogether. "Well, Ma," she said, "it doesn't sound as if it's shaping up to be one of your most successful affairs. I mean if Joe's mother's such a reluctant starter and if Pa insists on bringing Caroline along and you don't want her here, well I do sincerely think you should consider calling the whole thing off."

Both Beatrice and George loudly supported the motion, but Mrs Huntley stood up and began to clear the dishes. "I think I know what my duty is here, thank you Rachel. I have never yet been able to win an argument with your father, I admit this, so if he chooses to act irresponsibly I shall have to endure it and try to behave with dignity."

This is going to be the most abysmal night of our entire lives. Please God send an earthquake Friday night. No, send it today, let's get it over with.

The prospect of the disapproving and unintelligible Mrs Deladro, the unwelcome and unspeakable Caroline, the shameless and brazen Mac Huntley, and most of all, the noble and dignified Janet Huntley, depressed them all.

So deep was his distress that George helped Rachel to wash the dishes with no intimidation required at all. Rachel was impressed, as it usually took a great deal of hearty and persistent blackmail, brutality and coercion to bring together George and a piece of dirty china.

As he stacked the plates he whispered, "I solemnly swear I'm running away come Saturday. Now you remember I said this, Rach, it might be important at the trial."

"What trial, George? They don't fling you into gaol just for running away, and I won't tell, I promise. May join you in fact. This is going to be one dire night I know."

"Well honest, Rach, the way Ma there's been carrying

on, I might be forced to do a spot of the old GBH before I go."

"The old what?"

"You know. A bit of the old Grievous. And believe me, I never thought I'd live to see the day I'd want to start smacking my own mother around. But *you* ever see her act as crazy as this?"

Rachel thought back and had to admit that of all her mother's recent moods, this was the nadir. Even when her father had packed his suitcase and called them all into the dining room to say goodbye her mother had acted calmly. He had broken the news to her the day before of course, so she had had a small amount of time to decide which face to wear and how to act. They knew that she cried a lot at night — as indeed they all did — but she managed the days admirably, so that George's dismay now was understandable.

He scrunched up the tea towel, as was his fastidious habit, and stuffed it behind the handle of the oven door.

Hang it for once, you slobby little midget!

He spotted a dollop of spilt muesli on the floor, so tidily ground it in with the toe of his sneaker.

"All his fault. Uppin' and offin' like that. She wasn't too bad 'til he did that."

"I know."

"I know. I know," he mimicked. "Well I reckon you must be crazy too. Racing out there to visit him and that. Dunno how you can stand it. You're nuts."

"Yes, well George I know it must be difficult for you to understand. And pick that up, don't grind it in! But someone in this family has to keep in touch. You needn't think it's any pleasure for me to go pedalling all the way out there to that stupid farm every other Sunday, and put up with the rest of you picking on me for it. I only go because, well, to sort of keep a line of communication open . . ."

George widened his eyes in the irritating way he had.

"Well, we might need him one day, say if Ma got sick, well take this wedding for instance, and if no one's even speaking to him . . . I'm merely trying to act in a civilised way, that's all."

George widened his eyes again. "Oh, well then, if we're going to talk *civilised* include me out. So long."

He mooched out into the garden. Her mother was polishing the silver again, insisting that no one else could, or would, do it properly, so Rachel collected her bicycle and set off to the other side of town. She rehearsed her lines as she pedalled, and changed the script so often that by the time she was almost at her destination she was still unsure of what she was going to say, and at each intersection she was tempted to turn and go home again.

The old weatherboard cottage stood close to the road and a big new sign above the veranda said CRAFT CENTRE with a lot of dots and whorls and five-petalled flowers playing among the letters. Rachel stood looking at it for a while partly to give herself more time to compose her speech and partly to wonder at the rare eccentricity of the sign. The letters became smaller towards the end, but raggedly, so that there was no illusion of perspective involved. Each vowel was shorter and wider than the other letters, and both Cs were so heavily embellished that their identity was quite lost, they could have been Os, Gs, or Qs, and Rachel was rolling her tongue around Cwaft Cwentre when a voice from the front window called her name. She turned to see the friendly face of Mrs Walker, the chemist's wife.

"Hello, Rachel dear, admiring our sign? It's wonderfully cheerful, isn't it? Rose, Miss Follett, our famous artist-in-residence painted it for us. Come in and meet her."

Rachel was tempted to leap back on to her bike and

escape but Mrs Walker stood her ground and maintained steady and inexorable eye contact. "Come along, dear. Perhaps you could give us a hand for just a moment, we've been hoping that someone might turn up."

Oh sure, Mrs Walker. Great. I was looking for something to do.

She was met at the door by what could only be the famous artist-in-residence. Miss Follett was alarmingly tall and thin, with thick grey hair hanging down her back in a heavy plait, and big, dark, intense eyes that stared as if they had always to be judging perspectives and assessing colours. Rachel supposed that it was a handy way for an artist's eyes to look, but if the Cwaft Cwentre sign was any indication of talent then she also decided that Miss Follett had a long way to go. Mrs Walker introduced them and Miss Follett offered a very colourful hand to be shaken. Rachel told her that the new sign was very . . . bright, and Miss Follett glowed and said that it had been no trouble to her, since she was an Art teacher at a big school in the city, and loved to spend her holidays in the country, helping her friends. The friend she was helping this time was Mrs Walker, they'd been at school together, so nothing was too much trouble.

As she spoke the two ladies gently but determinedly steered their prey towards the back of the house. They entered a room where the floor around the walls was stacked with paintings of all sizes, the table in the centre was covered with a large and intricate diagram, and the chair was occupied by the Walkers' only child, Rachel's all-time least favourite person.

Bede Walker sat with his left leg in heavy plaster, his bandaged left arm in a sling, and his right eye glaring angrily at the newcomers. His left eye was closed and surrounded by a palette of such variegated tints as Miss Follett would have been proud to have produced.

"What are you doing here?"

"Brought home yesterday," Mrs Walker announced in a proud tone. She hadn't wanted Bede to go to the snow with the class in the first place, now she'd been proved right. "Invalided out, poor lamb."

"What happened?"

"Oh just practising some jumps and turns, pretty difficult stuff actually, the snow was dead treacherous. You know."

Oh sure, I'd know wouldn't I? Practically the only one out of the whole class who didn't go.

"According to Mr Lamb he was fooling about, collided with a tree. I *said* it was too dangerous down there." Mrs Walker turned to Miss Follett. "Rachel and Bede are chums at school, dear, just like we were."

You know I very much doubt that. Old Bede there with his very-well-deserved-I'm-sure wounds makes my life at school a living hell. Chums we are not.

"Well I'm sorry you busted yourself up, Bede. I've got to go now, Mrs Walker, just remembered, Mum asked me to do something."

The last thing Rachel's mother had asked her to do was to please go away and leave her in peace, but even returning home was preferable to spending time with the intolerable Bede. Mrs Walker, however, chose to ignore her and before Rachel knew what was going on she was on top of a set of steps attaching the awful paintings to studs on the canvas wall. Miss Follett handed them up to her and Bede sat morosely on his chair, consulting the diagram on the table and directing her where to put them.

After what seemed hours of this she was delighted to hear a familiar voice in the hallway and to see Caroline come into the room.

"Coffee time! Come on you slaves, time for a rest. Sorry I wasn't here when you came, Rachel, great to see you." Like sheep following their leader they all trooped into the room across the hall and filled their mugs at the coffee urn. All except Bede, but his mother trotted back with a cup for him, and the tin of biscuits for him to choose from.

That's right. Spoil him rotten. I really can't see what you find to like in that boy, Mrs Walker. He's a vicious twit.

"So you're at school with Bede. Rachel, is it? I really am so sorry, awfully bad at remembering names." Lofty Miss Follett hovered, grappling with her mug, a screw-topped jar half full of sugar, and a spoon. "Such a sweet boy, isn't he?"

"Yes." Rachel was too weary to argue, "Yes, he's sweet. Bede is sweet, Miss Follett." There was some satisfaction in the knowledge that Bede would die from embarrassment were he to hear himself described as "sweet", but she had no time to enjoy it. She had to talk to Caroline.

At last the others drifted out of the room and they were alone.

"Well, now you've seen the place, what do you think?" Caroline seemed anxious for a favourable report, so Rachel began, "Well, I think the sign's a bit, well . . ." Miss Follett's eager, slightly vacant face came into her mind. "It's good. I mean it's sort of amateurish, but that makes it sort of — charming, I guess."

"Yes, I do agree, it's terrible. You'd like to work here?"

"Yes. No. That's not why I came. Listen, Caroline. Ma telephoned Pa last night . . ."

"Yes I know. And I . . ."

"Please don't come. I mean, she's already got the dreaded Mrs Deladro to cope with, and *she* doesn't even want them to get married at all, poor old Beatrice. And Ma's got us all cleaning the house, and she doesn't know what to give them to eat, and George says he's going to run away."

Caroline took away Rachel's coffee cup and pushed her into a chair. "Sit down, take some slow, deep breaths, and relax, Rachel. Sounds like a gala dinner party, doesn't it? It seems to me I should come, if only to give a hand."

Rachel stared at her feet.

"Look, I'll talk to your father about it, eh? That's all I can offer at the moment. But whatever happens, it's not your fault, darling. Do relax. Now what about that job?"

Rachel stood up. "I'll think about it. See how things go. Can't decide right now. Okay? And *please* don't come."

And without saying goodbye to the others, she hurried out to her bicycle and pedalled back home.

6

It was Thursday morning and her mother was out shopping for the raw materials for Saturday's party.

Rachel was lonely, wishing that one of her friends had been invalided home from the snow instead of the noxious Bede. Any friend would do, and any friend of hers would cope with broken limbs far better than Bede was doing. She wandered through the house afraid to touch a thing in case some sort of preservation order had been placed on it, and finally decided that the kitchen was the safest place to be, since it was bound to be messed up a bit by food preparation in the next couple of days. She pondered escape-routes, recalled a story of an old guy who drank hemlock and wondered where you got it, was it irreversibly lethal, and what was the old guy's name. So she took the old and battered encyclopaedia with her and settled down at the kitchen table. The description of hemlock was interesting, and the writer advised her (in brackets) to see Socrates, and *that* was the name she'd been groping for. Socrates led her to Plato, and Plato to Ionia, and by that time she was so delighting in her fossicking that she decided she might as well tackle the whole of Greece. Architecture, Art, History, Language and Literature, with sidetracks leading off in all directions, kept her busy until George banged a mug of tea between her and the big book.

"Din even hear me come in, didya?" he accused. "Man comes home, says gizza cuppa tea. What's he get? Ignore. That's what he gets. Straight ignore. Gotta go make it hisself."

"Oh tough! I do apologise, I'm sure. MAN comes in, of COURSE the little woman should dash up and wait on him hand and foot. You're quite capable of making your own tea, George."

"I said, din I? Made you one too, din I? You don want it I'll tip it straight down the sink."

Rachel grabbed the mug. "Well there's no need to be so surly. Thank you most graciously for making me this delicious mug of tea. And just by way of sisterly instruction, 'ignore' happens to be a verb, so you can't get 'ignore'. Will you just try to remember that, so's you don't embarrass me by saying it some time in the future when people I know might hear you. I mean it sounds dead ignorant, Georgie."

"Don't call me ignorant. Don't call me Georgie. And don't worry about me embarrassing you in the future, Toots." He picked up his mug of tea, scooped a handful of biscuits from the tin, whacked the lid shut with his elbow, and marched out into the garden.

Sorry George love. I'll just finish this bit and then I'll come out and be nice to you.

But she left it too long, and was up another side road with Plutarch, and her tea was stone-cold when the front doorbell rang. She looked into the garden, and there was no sign of George, so to save extra steps on the shampooed carpets she walked around the side of the house to see who had come.

It was Beatrice's boyfriend, Joe Deladro, in tatty jeans and holey T-shirt with a large box of vegetables balanced on his shoulder. When he saw her he put the box down on the veranda table and advanced with open arms and a wide smile.

"Hi, Rach. Great news, eh? Our engagement? Aren't you thrilled?" He snatched her up and swung her around and gave her a loud and smacking kiss.

Do you mind? I've only met you twice!

"Sure. Thrilled. Great news. Would you mind putting me down now please. I've got this serious back complaint and you might be doing it irreversible harm."

"Hey, I didn't know that. Gee I'm sorry."

"Oh don't worry about it. Nothing really. We don't talk about it."

You hear that? We don't talk about it, so don't you start, will you, or I'll be in trouble. And with more than my back!

"Well here, you take it easy. Can I give these to your mum? My Uncle Angelo grows them, said for me to bring them over."

"You've got relatives here?"

"Sure. Three families of them, all farmers. Athelton's our nearest town actually, I only come here because of the college. Seventeen cousins I've got, and they're all looking forward to this wedding."

Seventeen cousins, say six uncles and aunts, and your mother. Makes for a pretty big wedding full of strangers. Ma will *be thrilled.*

She took him into the kitchen with his box, and had to admit the vegetables did look fresh and succulent. Then to avoid a private conversation, she bellowed for George. He emerged finally from the storeroom at the end of the back veranda, looking sheepish. Ashamed of his earlier crankiness, Rachel supposed.

"So," he began, as the three of them sat around the kitchen table, "so, you're planning to marry my sister."

He sounded so much like a stern Victorian father having to interview a brash prospective son-in-law that Rachel grinned. She looked up, and caught Joe grinning too.

Watch it, buster.

"I'll make us all a cup of coffee," she said.

"That'd be great," Joe smiled.

No it wouldn't. We've only got instant, and Italians drink the real stuff.

"On second thoughts, we usually take tea at this time of day."

"Okay."

She decided that Beatrice's Joe didn't have much guts, he'd obviously agree to anything, and she hurried off to the dining room to fetch the silver tray and tea-service and the best cups and saucers. George gaped when he saw them, but he was doing his best to exclude her from the conversation, so didn't comment. She made the tea, took the tin of biscuits off the table and arranged a few on one of her mother's Royal Doulton plates.

"This looks very classy," Joe commented.

"Classy? You mean the tea-service? Oh, it's quite ordinary really. We use it all the time. Would you care for a biscuit?"

She managed to pry the plate from George's protective grasp while carefully avoiding his goggling eyes and slack jaw.

"Beatrice says you're studying computers and that sort of thing," she murmured, feeling a bit as if she had taken over the role of Victorian parent herself.

"Computers and that sort of thing just about covers it I suppose," Joe agreed. "No lectures today, so I'm helping the rels with the crops. Why don't you both come out to see the farms some time? My Uncle Angelo grows grapes, makes his own wine. You'd love it."

George was about to leap to his feet and set off right

away, but Rachel, not knowing why, set her cup down carefully in its saucer and murmured, "Perhaps later, if you and Beatrice marry, we'll meet your relatives."

"I'll come," George rebelled at last. But Joe put his cup down too and stood up.

"We'll check with your mother, eh George? If it's okay with her you're welcome any time. I'd better get back to work now. Thanks for the, ah, hospitality." He flicked a quick smile at Rachel and was gone.

She carried the cups and plates to the sink one by one and George watched, turning his head deliberately as she moved.

"Will you stop staring at me?"

"When you tell me why you did that."

"Did what?"

"Oh, come off it, Rachel. Whyd'ya talk to him like that for? And the best plates and stuff for cryin' out loud! Talk about showing off! Blimey! He's not a bad sort of bloke."

"You think he's good enough for Bea? He's a yobbo, that's what he is, a burly, big yobbo. She's too young to get married anyway, and he's not, she's not, I don't . . ."

Oh God, if you let me cry in front of this infant that's the last time you get my vote. I'll join the infidels I swear.

"Perhaps later, IF you and Beatrice marry, we'll meet your relatives." He'd always been an expert mimic and he got her voice and intonation just right. But this time it had the advantage of making her so mad that tears were no longer to be considered.

"Well, if Beatrice likes him, that's her problem, but we don't have to encourage him."

"You don't have to be so careful washing those plates. 'They're quite ordinary really. We use them all the time.' Just wait to hear what Ma's got to say about that!"

"Here, have another biscuit, George. Have three."

George took three and stuffed them into an already

bulging shirt pocket. Then he took another and stuffed that into his mouth. Rachel stacked the china and the silver tea-service back on to the tray and sat down opposite him.

"Look, George," she said in a very reasonable tone of voice. "I've got nothing against Joe. Really I haven't. I hardly know him, so how could I? All I want is for B to find a wonderful husband and be happy. Don't you?"

George nodded seriously and absorbed another biscuit.

"Yes, we all do. Well, if Joe's the one and IF they get married, then I'll be delighted for both of them. But in the meantime, I reckon it's best if we don't act too enthusiastic."

"Whysat?" George enquired through biscuit crumbs.

She wanted to explain that she was only acting as a sort of devil's advocate, but she'd only recently found the term in the *Dictionary of Idioms*, and wasn't sure enough of her ground to test it with a skilled inquisitor like George.

"Listen, George, you'll just have to trust me on this one." Then she played her trump card, and ignored her feelings of guilt as she laid it on the table between them. "You realise that Ma was just twenty when she married Pa, don't you?"

He nodded, chewing no longer.

"Well she was too immature and you know what happened to their marriage. How unhappy she is. You wouldn't want to be responsible for that happening to Bea, would you?"

He shook his head, looking so miserable and young that she delved into the biscuit tin and found a chocolate one for him.

"Here. Cheer up. It's not the end of the world, duck. It's just that I think you and I should go carefully, you know, not go overboard. Then if things work out, fine; if they don't, then they can't blame us for anything, can they?"

"Ma'll blame you all right, you smash one of her best cups." He sniffed loudly. Rachel hated the sound of George's sniffs, but this time she let it go. "Okay, well, I'll go along with that. I won't let on to Ma about this stuff either, but you better put it away before she gets home. By the way. You seen that little billy can we used to take camping?"

Rachel paused on her way to the dining room with the tray.

"On the top shelf in the store room. Why? What do you want it for?"

"Might go yabbying this arvo." George ducked out the door as they heard their mother's car turning into the driveway.

"He seems a very thoughtful boy," Mrs Huntley mused as she stowed broccoli in the crisper and potatoes in the drawer. "I do hope things work out well for them. What did you talk about when he came?"

Well there was my bad back, and the prodigal way we use the good china, and doubts about their wedding ever coming off. Just idle chat like that. Ma, you'd kill me if I told you.

"Oh nothing. His course, things like that. He's got an Uncle Angelo, the one who grew this lot. Grows grapes and makes wine." She decided that the glad tidings that Joe had seventeen cousins all down on their starting blocks ready to come to the wedding should be kept for another time.

"That's interesting. Now I've decided against a buffet — too elaborate, we don't want to make it too grand."

No, don't want to scare the hell out of old Ma Deladro I guess.

"I'll make it a simple meal, almost potluck. I'm doing the Burgundy Beef tonight, that's best if it keeps for a couple of days. You could help me with that if you wouldn't mind, Rachel. We might do the ice-cream bombe early as well, let the brandy soak in to the fruit.''

Some potluck!

But Rachel was glad that her mother's preoccupation with the dinner party was making her lose interest in normal conversation, otherwise more questions about Joe's visit might have been asked. So she mutely chopped vegetables and meat. Mrs Huntley coped with the ice-cream bombe, and George, as soon as he'd finished his meal, disappeared until bedtime.

7

"Wow, this sure is an alcoholic meal, Ma." Rachel lifted the lid off the burgundy beef and sniffed appreciatively.

"It's too much, isn't it? Yes, too alcoholic. I should have made something else. Well it's not too late. I'll make something else."

She gnawed at a fingernail for a moment, then darted across to the shelf where the cookery books lived. As her mother began to flick the pages, hoping that the perfect recipe would leap into sight, Rachel realised what a risky remark she had made. Visions came to her of horses being changed in midstream, more shopping, more cooking, more cleaning, barges to be lifted, bales to be toted. . . .

"No! Listen, Ma. I meant it's great. I mean being so alcoholic, that's great. You can tell that pâté's been hit, wow! and Pa loves your Burgundy Beef, we all do, and that bombe with the brandied fruit! I reckon you couldn't do better at the poshest restaurant in the world. This'll be the best dinner you've put on. Ever. I mean it."

"Well you're sure it's not too much? There's green salad as well, and the rice of course, and my pumpkin soup to start with. There's no alcohol in that. Well, just a dash of sherry. What do you *really* think, Rachel?"

"Spot on, Ma. That's what I think, really. Sounds a great meal, just highlighted with the few little drops of grog."

She quickly shut the door of the refrigerator before the heady fumes from the few little drops of grog could send her reeling around the room and ricocheting off the furniture.

"Yep. Spot on."

Her mother settled, but retained the distracted eyes and the tight-lipped mouth that she wore so often these days.

"Yes, well I'll leave it then. Now I've got to make the soup, check the table linen, have my hair set, that's in the morning. Flowers! I forgot the flowers!"

"No you didn't. You rang Daisy Rose this morning. Is that her real name do you think?"

"What? Oh darling, I'm sorry. Why don't you go off and visit one of your friends . . . Oh, they're all at the snow, aren't they . . . No of course it's not. Her real name is much worse than that, poor thing. I just forget what it is at the moment."

"Okay, Ma, I'm off. I'll leave you in peace until about four."

And boy, do I wish tomorrow night was over already!

As she collected her bike from the storeroom she saw that George had already taken his out and wondered where he'd gone. Even George's company might help to pass the time.

She loitered at the bus-stop hoping to see Beatrice and was rewarded. Her sister's smooth blonde hair hovered behind the closed door, the bus stopped and the hair swung heavily as she turned to thank the driver. Then the door opened and she emerged, leaving the poor driver grinning vacantly as he groped for the gears.

She even looks like an angel. Or a princess. Not one of

your now *princesses. A fairy-story princess, that's what she looks like. What's she want to go and get married for?*

"Hi. I've been banished while Ma gets on with her panicking. Come for a ride?"

But Beatrice had an assignment to finish, so Rachel mounted the bicycle and set off down the road alone. Suddenly she was outside the Craft Centre, with no memory at all of pedalling in that direction, but filled with fervent hope that the insufferable Bede might be somewhere else.

He wasn't. The moment she set food inside the door she heard his monotonous drone emanating from the back room. He seemed to be giving careful and detailed instructions to someone on the various methods of stopping a downhill run on skis. Rachel decided that he was hardly qualified to do that, so she hurried down the hallway to tell him so.

Sure enough, there he was again, or still, ensconced on his chair flaunting his plaster and bandages while angular Rose Follett stood behind him massaging his neck. Rachel wondered for a moment about the ethics of pointing out his shortcomings, with him being practically a cripple, then she decided that the Rose Folletts of this world need some protection from those who can give it, against the Bede Walkers who infest the planet.

"Hey, Bede," she therefore said, "if you know so much about skiing, how come you came such a bad cropper yourself? Eh?"

But instead of shame and embarrassment on the part of Bede and gratitude from Miss Follett, all she gained from her righteous reproof was a tolerant smile from both of them. Bede lurched off to be driven home by his mother, and Miss Follett insisted on making coffee. Rachel felt small and flattened, particularly since there was no sign of Caroline and she was reluctant to ask about her. But Miss Follett handed her the hot mug and settled down on the other chair, and looked so friendly and somehow as if she was waiting to be told, and there was a silence that needed to be filled, so Rachel began to tell her.

"I just don't know what's wrong with Ma. I mean, I don't want to be disloyal and that." Miss Follett's expression assured her that it wouldn't be disloyal to just talk about it for a while. "There's this dinner tomorrow, hits off with the chicken liver pâté, stiff with alcohol, and she's doing her Burgundy Beef, *and* this bombe thing that just reeks of brandy, plus there's the pumpkin soup with the dollop of cream on top and a slurp of sherry, and honestly, Miss Follett, they'll all drop dead of raging indigestion, 'cept for George of course, he'll eat anything. And it's not even that it's so rich. It's more than she can't stop. She's trying to impress people. Caroline, and Joe's mother. It's going to be the most mortifying event in my entire life. And if you say a word she jumps on you. I tell you, Miss Follett, Ma's a changed woman since Pa left."

Miss Follett put down her mug; typically she had taken the most battered one with the cracks and chips and the broken handle.

"You know dear," she murmured, "I think your poor mother might be feeling a trifle under par at the moment."

"Oh no, she's a very healthy person. We all are."

"Physically, of course, but . . . Oh, there's Caroline. I expect you came to see her. I'll just clear up in the studio."

And she tactfully departed, knocking over and picking up just about every article of furniture in the room as she went. Rachel felt a vague disappointment. While she and Miss Follett had sat together at the old table, she had experienced a strange feeling of being safe, and at peace, warm, and forgiven.

Forgiven? For what? What have I done? It's her eyes, she's a hypnotist, that's what it is.

She didn't feel like discussing her mother's state with Caroline, who was quite adamant about the party.

"Your father won't go without me. Your mother needs him there. He should be there. Ergo, I shall be there. Sorry, dear, I know it's tough, but life is tough. Now are you coming to work here or not?"

"Not. Thanks anyway. I've organised something else. 'Bye."

As she slowly pedalled down the main street she wondered why she had turned down a perfectly good paying job. Something to do with those eyes of Miss Follett? A suspicion that working with Caroline might seem disloyal to her mother?

Nope. Just I reckon there's too many Bede Walkers around that Craft Centre these days. Don't need the money anyway.

But she was passing Mr Walker's chemist shop right then, and the glamorous and gorgeous Sandra flashed into her mind.

Better check with George. He might come in on a car-wash business with me. Lawn-mowing? Dog walking?

But George's scorn was magnificent to see. "Dog mowing? Lawn washing, and what was the other one? Oh yeah, car walking. No thanks. Not innerested. Wouldn't mind having a chat with this Uncle Angelo bloke, give him a hand making that wine. Hey, borrow your bike lamp? Might go see *The Maltese Falcon* tonight, and my batteries are low."

"Great! I'll come with you, if Ma springs the money for the tickets. I figure this is a good night to be out of the house."

But George was adamant. He wouldn't be seen dead going to the pictures with a sister. He hadn't finally decided to go. She wouldn't like the movie, and anyway, he'd promised to go with old Whiffy Baker if he went at all. That put her off, Whiffy was notorious for the way he could enter a room and empty it of people in no time at all. A night at the Embassy would be unbearable in the presence of the old Whiff. Lonely too, as the other patrons slunk out one by one with their noses averted. But Rachel lent the bicycle lamp anyway; George was looking quite peaky these days, so she gave his shoulder a squeeze as she passed, and was surprised at how frail it felt under her hand.

"Hey, Rach . . ." he began, but she had to hurry inside to decide with Beatrice what they were both wearing to the party.

"Catch up with you later, George," she called as she crossed the veranda, and she really did mean to.

George stood for a moment looking after her, then he kicked the veranda post, turned, and walked slowly away.

8

It was seven-fifteen. The food was ready, the table laid, they were all dressed and waiting for the first guests to come. And George was missing.

At first Rachel was the only one who knew. Her mother and Beatrice were busy measuring the distance the wineglasses should stand from the knives, and folding the table napkins in such a way that the embroidered bits all faced the same direction, so that they failed to notice the absence of a small brother and son. She wondered if she should tell them, or let the fact dawn on them gradually, thus being less of a shock perhaps? Then her mother, about to arrange the flowers in the bowl on the dining table just one more time, glanced around and said, "Where's George?"

"Oh honestly!" Beatrice wailed. "That boy! I *told* him to have another shower and get dressed hours ago."

"Yes, well you know how he hates having showers, Beatrice dear, and two in one day! Possibly you could have compromised with a good wash. See if he's still in the bathroom, Rachel. He locked himself in there for three hours once just because your father commented on his fingernails. Only said you could grow a great crop of potatoes in there, and George took umbrage. But he did emerge when lunchtime came around I remember.''

"He's not in the bathroom,'' said the returning Rachel.

"He'll be somewhere,'' his mother insisted with awesome wisdom. "He'll come as soon as dinner's served. You wait and see.''

"He's not anywhere in the house,'' Rachel whispered, feeling a strange numbness invading her body. "I've looked everywhere, Ma.''

Beatrice, being older, went to look everywhere herself, and Mrs Huntley continued to pat the flowers into place and to brush imaginary crumbs from the immaculate tablecloth.

"Ma. Look at me. He's not here. Did you say he could go to the movies tonight?''

"What do you mean? I certainly wouldn't have let him go anywhere with all these people coming. He's here somewhere. I'm sure he's here. Would you look around outside? No, I'll go. George! Where are you, you little monster. My word you're in for a beating when I find you. Just wait until I tell your father . . .''

Her voice faded as she went outside. Rachel's stomach was leaden and her chest ached. She knew that George was nowhere about. Beatrice came back, convinced, and angry.

"He's doing this deliberately to spoil my party and when he turns up I'm going to wallop the hell out of him. You hear me?''

At that moment the doorbell rang and Mrs Huntley came flying in from outside.

"Don't say anything about this, girls,'' she gasped, "he'll be back. Probably popped around to see that smelly friend of his. Bike's gone, so that's where he'll be. Come along now.''

They each paused for a moment at the mirror in the hall,

then Mrs Huntley opened the door and faced her errant husband and "that woman".

He, smiling firmly and seeming quite oblivious to any reason for embarrassment, gave hugs and kisses all round which his forsaken daughters and discarded wife accepted, partly from habit but also from a reluctance to spurn his affection, so guilelessly offered.

Realising that once more she had allowed his charm to catch her off-guard, Janet tightened up her face and nodded to Caroline. Beatrice smiled at all the world, hoping that Joe would soon arrive, and Rachel wondered, not for the first time, how her father managed to get away with it. She took the bottles of champagne he'd brought and put them in the refrigerator, then opened the back door and hissed "George, hey George, come on home will you?"

Then, as the pain in her chest prodded and fear nudged at her she ran across the lawn to the trees where the old cubby perched. She had already looked there, and her brain told her quite definitely that George was nowhere near the house. Still, she stood and called softly into the unresponding branches.

"Please come back, Georgie-Porge. It'll be all right. I promise. Truly."

"Rachel, the Deladros are here." Her mother's voice called from the doorway, and her mother's hand patted her arm as she passed inside. "He'll be back, dear. It's just after seven. He's forgotten about the party, probably watching television with that boy Smelly."

"It's Whiffy, Ma. Listen. I think he might have run away."

Oh hell, there I go. Can't I keep a worry to myself just this once? Now her face'll fall to pieces.

But Mrs Huntley was determined not to show her worry, at least not until the formalities had been attended to properly. She kept her face intact and led Rachel in to meet Joe's mother. And that took thoughts of George out of her head for a while. Thoughts of everything in fact. Mrs Deladro was tall, taller even than Caroline, with light red hair and eyes unexpectedly brown. Her figure was spectacular, and that plus the proficiency of her make-up caused poor Sandra from the pharmacy to lose her crown and be forgotten immediately. Even her name was a song.

"Pa-oola. I am Pa-oola." Her voice was husky and it fitted in so well with the rest of her that Rachel stood mesmerised.

"Pa-oola," she breathed. "I'm Rachel. How do you spell that?"

Joe grinned. "It's P-A-O-L-A. Paula here I guess, or Pauline. Mamma keeps the Italian way of pronouncing it."

"Well, she's entitled, isn't she? I mean, it's her name."

"Oh sure." He came closer. "How's your bad back, Rachel? You should be sitting down, resting it, shouldn't you?" Her mother was fetching chicken pâté and biscuits from the kitchen and Beatrice was mooning at Joe from across the room while she talked to her father and Caroline. The devil in Rachel spoke.

"Paola Deladro. It's a lovely name. Now the 'de' part means 'of' doesn't it? And 'ladro', I just can't remember . . ." *Didn't think we'd have an Italian dictionary in the house, did you, Joe?*

Mrs Deladro smiled, evidently comprehending little of Rachel's barb. Joe grinned.

"Means robber, thief, that's what *ladro* means in Italian. So I come of a line of thieves and felons, don't I Rachel? I hope your mother's hidden the good silver."

Listen, Joe. George's run away. What'll we do?

"You have a large family here, Mrs Deladro?"

Why am I acting like this? She looks all right. Help!

"When my husband die last year we come to live with his brother on farm." Mrs Deladro seemed comfortable talking about her abundance of relatives and was down to describing, in English that was hard to understand but melodious to listen to, Joe's eleventh cousin, when at precisely the same moment Mrs Huntley announced that dinner was served and Mr Huntley said, "Where's George?"

"Out," his wife announced in a dismissive tone. Implying that since she had been left to bring up the child, she was the one to know where he was, his father the one to find out. "Would you all come now, please?"

They straggled in to the dining room and for a while it seemed like a mad game of musical chairs as Mrs Huntley changed her mind about where each should sit and her husband and Joe dashed about pulling out chairs for the women who bobbed up and down like yoyos at her command. At last they were settled and Rachel helped her mother distribute the soup. When it had been consumed in a self-conscious silence, she gathered the empty plates. Quickly she dumped them on the kitchen bench, then snatched the telephone from the wall and flicked the pages of the book of numbers that her mother kept nearby. Damn, no number for Baker. She sneaked back along the hallway, past the door to the dining room, relieved to hear her father telling one of his interminable stories, to the hall phone and its book. She dialled the number and breathily asked Mrs Baker if George had been sighted. He had not, and Damien (Whiffy? *Damien*?) was watching television completely alone.

Sorry Ma. I think I'm now about to deliver the final knockout blow to this party.

She stood in the doorway of the dining room looking at them: Beatrice and Joe surreptitiously holding hands under the table; Mrs Huntley smiling, a happy hostess if it killed her, and it possibly would; Caroline and Mrs Deladro obviously wanting to be somewhere else, and Mr Huntley still on his story, doing his best to play the genial host.

Listen everyone. It's George. He's run away. I know he has. Said he would. We've got to do something. He'll be so frightened. He hates the dark.

Her mother looked up and saw her lingering forlornly by the door. "Come on, darling," she said briskly, "I'll help you with the rest." And she quickly steered Rachel in to the kitchen.

"Ma, it's George."

"Yes, I know, dear. I'm worried about him too."

"He's not with Whiffy Baker, I telephoned."

"Well it must be the cinema. He's been talking all week about *The Maltese Falcon* being on and I *said* he'd have to wait until after tonight. Then of course, he's been very upset about your father. Look, darling, if we tell the others he'll be even more upset when he does come home, so you ring the Embassy and ask if they've seen him there. They certainly must know him, he practically haunts the place. I'll get this ready."

Rachel could see that her mother was really worried now, and more about the whereabouts of George than about the success of her party. So she left her standing by the oven, sucking a burned finger, and advanced once more on the telephone in the hallway.

"Sure he's here. So's every other twelve-year-old lives in this town. You want to come and fetch him home you're more than welcome, love. Take the lot far's I'm concerned. My treat."

But Love was not satisfied. "Are you sure, though? His name's George Huntley, he's not very tall for his age, and he's got dark brown, sort of wavy hair, pretty long, and brown eyes and a sort of olive complexion. He'd have a bicycle chained up outsi . . ."

"Ain't they all got bikes cluttering up the footpath? Ain't they all got long hair? He'd be one of this lot for sure."

"Do you think you could announce his name over the speaker thing, like when you ask if there's a doctor in the house?"

"Listen, I ain't *never* asked if there was a doctor in the house. Why'd I do that? No doctors don't come near this dump. Only kids. And I gotta go settle another fight."

"Wait! When you're doing that, settling the fight I mean, couldn't you just call out, is George Huntley here, and if he says he is, come and tell me? No, you couldn't could you. What time does the show finish?"

She crept back to the kitchen. Her mother had not moved from the oven door; she was still sucking her finger.

"Show finishes ten-thirty. I reckon he must be there, Ma. He did talk about going yesterday. Look, don't worry. The man says he thinks he saw him there. I described him pretty well."

Oh George, why do you have to be so ordinary. We need some distinguishing features, dammit.

They carried the Burgundy Beef and the hot rice, the plates and the big bowl of green salad back in to the dining room, where silence had fallen again.

9

To fill an awkward gap Beatrice told the table that the Deladros had come from Verona. She said it proudly, as if Verona could now lay claim to being the centre of the universe.

"Two Gentlemen of . . ." Mr Huntley beamed, just as proud of being the literary lion of the family.

"And Romeo and Juliet," his wife spoke up gallantly, trying to keep the conversational ball in play.

"For the *touristi* perhaps," Mrs Deladro said. "For me, is more famous for Dante Alighieri, Paolo Veronese."

End of that conversational gambit.

But Caroline deftly caught the ball and tossed it back. "I've been to Verona," she said, "there's an enormous coliseum there, and a beautiful open-air theatre and a museum on a hill across the river. Am I right, Paola?"

Wrong!

"The coliseum's in Rome, isn't it?"

"I guess Rome's might be the biggest, but a lot of towns have them. There's a big one in Arles too."

The mention of Arles seemed to cast a blight on both senior Huntleys, as well as on Caroline, but in her agitated state Rachel pressed on.

"That's in France, isn't it? Arles? How long were you there, you lucky duck?"

"A long time. She lived there a long time." Her father glared across the table, then lifted his glass. "Now let's get down to the real business of the evening. A toast to the bride and groom to be."

And *that* didn't please Mrs Deladro too much, either. She took a reluctant sip of her wine, put her glass down, and went back to pushing pieces of beef around and around her plate. But Mac Huntley had had enough. Years of handling staff in the general store had given him an air of authority, along with a short fuse.

"Now," he said, "we seem to have a problem here. Why are you all so glum? You first, Paola (pronouncing it carefully, so as not to contribute more to the evening's miseries). You don't seem very happy about this engagement. Got something against my daughter? Speak up, you're among friends."

Mrs Deladro made it short and sharp. "My son is Catholic," she said.

All eyes turned to Joe, who shrugged as if his religion was a condition quite beyond his ability to control, and said nothing. Beatrice kept the smile pasted on her face, showing the party that this discussion had nothing at all to do with her either.

"So?" her father persisted.

"Is not good that he marry out."

Joe then came to life. "Mamma, admit it. You want me to go back to Italy, to fair Verona, choose a fair Veronese to marry. That's what you want, isn't it?"

His mother turned on him, and Rachel realised why people said that red hair was synonymous with fiery temper.

"*Si,* Guiseppe, I admit. And why not? Twelve years I live in this country, I come because your father want a better chance for you. But what do I have? What life do I have? We live in the city, you have your school, your Australian friends, your father have his job, his Australian friends. I work in factory, with other Italian women. I have no Australian friends. All I have is my religion. It save my sanity at the beginning. Then your father die. What can I do?"

"But the uncles, they all wanted you to come . . ."

"Do I have a choice? I *want* to go back to Italy, to my 'fair Verona' like you say. I have no money to do that. So I put my hopes in my son. And at age twenty-two he decide he want to be marry."

She glared across at poor Beatrice, who wilted.

"No degree yet, no job. He help his uncles on their farms, we live on their charity, and he decide he want to be marry."

Rachel sneaked a glance at her watch. It was almost nine-thirty. Her father, with all the finesse of a bull among fine china, lumbered into the argument.

"Paola, dear, we can probably give a hand there. I've got this business in town you see. Family thing, badly needs good staff. I can give the lad a job tomorrow."

Whoops, Pa.

"My son is study to be scientist. I no want him work in your shop. Our family will support him until he has degree, then he get a *real* job. Without impediments."

Beatrice, the chief impediment, looked ready to weep. Janet, with the unexpected alliance of Caroline, rose to clear the plates. Rachel eagerly joined them.

"Look," she said when they had gained the sanctuary of the kitchen. "I think I'll just nip down to the Embassy and check if George is there. I don't want any of the ice-cream bombe, and I won't be gone long. They'll never miss me in there, anyway."

Then Caroline had to be brought up to date on the

mystery of George's disappearance. She surprised Rachel by walking across the room and putting her arm around Mrs Huntley's shoulder.

"How worried you must be," she said, "but I don't think Rachel should go alone, do you, Janet? Why not let Mac drive her down in the car, be quicker, meantime the two of us might have a chance of defusing the situation in there. Eh?"

Mrs Huntley nodded. "I would feel happier if I knew where he was. Come on, dear, we'll tell your father."

Mr Huntley, way out of his depth in the argument, was happy to accompany Rachel to the cinema, so they set off.

"Attractive woman that, but a bit of a tartar, eh? How was I to know her Guiseppe was such a brain. Only met him tonight! Thought he might *like* to work in the store. *Some* people like working there. I know I don't, but *some* people seem to. Old Beatrice'd better pull up her socks, might have some mother-in-law problems, don't you reckon, Rach?"

"I'm on her side, actually. A, they're too young to be getting married, B, different religions, that means trouble, and C, well, he's Italian, she's Australian. Makes problems."

"Rubbish! C, he's an Australian, it's his mother who's set on staying Italian. B, what's different religions got to do with it? Lots of people have different religions, bit of commonsense and tolerance is all that's needed there. Bit of the old give and take. And A, as for A, my girl. Do you realise that Beatrice and Joe are just the same age, exactly, that your mother and I were when we were married?"

Bad argument, Pa.

"Well, guess that's not much of an argument, is it? But I think they'll be all right. I like young Joe, and B's got a good head on her shoulders. Here we are."

There must have been twenty bicycles chained along the

footpath outside the Embassy, and George's was not among them. Rachel went up and down the line to check them out, then followed her father through the glass doors into the lobby. A tall, untidy man approached; by his wild eye and harassed manner Rachel judged him to be the same person she had spoken to on the telephone earlier.

"What a night!" He complained. "And this is Bogart! We got a horror festival coming up and I tell you here and now, I'm resigning before that starts. Otherwise they carry me off on a stretcher. Help you?"

After Mr Huntley had explained the problem, he sighed deeply, collected his torch from the ledge by the ticket-office, and led them through the green padded door into the theatre. Up and down the aisles they went, with the torch lighting up the faces of the audience. Some — enraptured Bogart fans — were watching the movie, but fights were going on in the front rows among the younger patrons, and the unruly situation at the back made Rachel decide that the manager was wise to resign before the horror festival began. He had obviously chosen the wrong job for his tender sensibilities.

Anxiously they stared at the face of each young boy in every row, and George was definitely not in the cinema. They thanked the man and walked slowly back to the car.

"Police," her father said. "We'll have to go to the police, child." Suddenly he sounded a hundred years old. He started the car up and drove slowly along the main street. Rachel peered out of her window, willing George to emerge from the dim shadows of a shop doorway, to wobble towards them on his bicycle, to call from the footpath, with an explanation, any explanation, no explanation.

Her father stopped the car in front of the police station and together they went in to the counter where the man on duty was drinking coffee and writing in a large book.

He was kind, and listened patiently to their tale, then

told them that the patrol car was out at the moment, dealing with "a domestic", and when it came back there was closing time at the hotels to be supervised, making it all seem much more urgent than the search for George.

"You notice anything missing from the house? Money? Clothing?"

Rachel remembered checking the storeroom when she first noticed his absence. "His bike, and my bike lamp. Said his battery was getting flat."

"Think," her father urged. "You're standing in the doorway of the storeroom. Everything there?"

"No! The shelf above the bikes! He took his sleeping-bag, and that old rucksack of yours. That's all I noticed. Didn't think to check on clothes and money. But he's *never* got any money . . ." Her voice trailed off as she realised that the policeman was implying that George had nicked someone else's money.

"He wouldn't steal." She spoke firmly and with confidence. "He always borrows, but he never steals." She felt tears prickle at her eyes, remembering how grudgingly she always lent her belongings to George, and how scrupulous he always was in giving them back, and how tatty they usually were when he did.

"Well then, see what I mean?" The policeman nodded; this sort of thing happened in his job all the time. "The lad's run away from home. They all do it once in a while. He'll be back, soon's he's ready for one of his mum's square meals. Probably gone with a friend. They usually go with a friend. I'd check out the friends, if I was you. He's not back in a day or two, get in touch with us. School holidays, see. They all run away in the school holidays."

Rachel could see hundreds of small boys scurrying off in all directions as the bell rang for the last day of school. And her George was definitely not one of them. "Come on, Pa," she said, "let's check out the friends."

"We'll certainly keep an eye out for the lad though," the policeman called as they went out the door to the car.

"Only friend he's got is Whiffy. Others've all gone off on holidays and things. Whiffy Baker. Real name's Damien. I'll show you."

The Bakers' house stood in a small yard full of luxuriant weeds, with the remains of an old half-buried car serving as a centrepiece. Lights were on, so Mr Huntley rapped on the scarred front door, and it was soon opened by Mrs Baker who went very well, Rachel thought, with the house and its setting. Damien was still up of course, watching television, to judge by the sounds that emanated from a room at the back of the house. His mother, after a few suspicious questions, sent him out to speak to them.

"Whiffy," Rachel began, deciding to start on a familiar note in hopes of gaining his confidence.

"Damien!" Her father interrupted indignantly. "The lad's name is Damien, Rachel."

"Whiffy's okay. They all call me Whiffy. It's 'cause I sweat a lot. Like when I'm nervous."

"Well there's no need to be nervous now, son."

No, Whiffy, please, please try not to be nervous.

"Have you seen George today?"

"Nope. Well, not to talk to anyway."

"So you saw him, but not to talk to?"

"Nope. Never seen him."

"Whiffy. Now think hard. But don't get nervous. When was the last time you did see George? At all, to talk to or not?"

"What you want to know for?"

"Well, we think he might've run away."

Whiffy, who had been leaning casually against the doorpost, was now galvanised into action.

"Who told you about running away?" he hissed. "I'm the one's running away. Soon's I save up me fare. Who told you? That George told you — I'll total him, that's what I'll do."

Rachel detected a clue. "No, George didn't tell us, we didn't know about your plans, but where are you running away to, Whiffy?"

"Me gran's. Lives down the city. Lets you do things, she does. Like smoking and that, and sitting up all night watching the telly, going up the Cross, things like that. Reckon she'd let me drink beer too, me Gran would, I wanted to. She does, like a fish. My old lady there, she makes you be in bed by twelve, and talk about scream if a person lights up a fag! Now she's stopped smoking, it's everyone stop smoking. Cheese!"

Mr Huntley was staring in disbelief at his son's best friend, but Rachel, recognising bravado when she saw it, asked calmly, "Which part of the city does she live in, your Gran?"

"Moves around. It's them landlords, see. Soon's she moves in a place they start wanting rent and that. Say she's gotta clean it up. Hassle. You know."

Obviously George had not fled to Whiffy's slovenly grandma. He'd be unable to track her down.

"Well good luck then, with your running away. Thanks."

"Hey, you won't go squealing to my old lady, willya?"

They both promised, solemnly, and as they backed off the rickety veranda the little boy called after them.

"Hey, that old George. He okay, is he?"

"Sure. He's okay, Whiffy. We'll be in touch."

Mrs Deladro was contrite, and Joe anxious to leave when they arrived back at the house. No one could tackle the ice-cream bombe, which was slowly subsiding into a puddle of wet fruit on the bottom of its specially chosen silver salver. Mrs Huntley made fresh coffee, and was so distraught that she forgot to count the spoonsful as she put them into the maker, and it was so strong that Beatrice had to throw it all away and make instant, herself too distraught to think of just adding water to dilute it.

Then Joe and his mother left, and Mr Huntley took over.

"Now, Janet, I want you to check George's room. See what clothes he took with him, and you might also find if there's any money missing. Give us an idea of how long he plans to be away. Rachel, I want you to look at that storeroom again. Did he take that small tent perhaps? The gas cooker?"

"Pa! He went on a bicycle! How could he manage the tent? And that cooker weighs a ton!" But she went, and found that the only things missing from the storeroom were the bicycle, his sleeping-bag, the rucksack, and her bike-lamp.

"He'd have to make a couple of trips with that lot, so he can't have gone far, can he?"

Beatrice announced that the large torch had gone (the one they kept by the stove in case of emergencies), also a plate and mug from the picnic set, a large tin of kippers (George's favourite food) and one of baked beans (also George's favourite food). George's liking for food was such that the distance between finishers in that race was quite impossible to gauge.

"Probably took bread as well, and fruit, and possibly some muesli, and yes, the old can-opener's gone. Look, it seems to me that he's only planned to be away overnight. He would have taken loads of stuff if he'd really meant to go a long way and stay a while. You know how he eats."

Indeed they did, and when Mrs Huntley reported that no money seemed to be missing, and that she really couldn't tell if he'd taken any extra clothes, but she didn't think he had, they were all relieved, and decided to let George have his little adventure and pay for it in the morning when he came home again.

When he came home again.

10

After her father and Caroline had driven away, Rachel closed the door and worked out her plan for the night. As soon as the others were asleep she would set out on her bicycle, quietly, and lampless of course thanks to George, find the little crumb and drag him squealing back home.

Beatrice, clearing up in the kitchen, was planning the same sort of exercise, but their mother took control straight away. She swept in from the dining room bearing a bottle of port in one hand and three small glasses cleverly held between the fingers of the other.

"Leave that," she commanded, "plenty of time to clear up this mess tomorrow. Now we're going to sit down quietly and have a glass of port together."

Henny-Penny that sky of yours has finally fallen!

"Me too, Ma? You mean you're planning to pour me a glass of that stuff from that bottle and actually let me drink it?"

Her mother laughed. "Darling, this is a special occasion, and I want to talk to you both." She poured the drinks and they sat around the kitchen table. Rachel took a sip and decided that port was probably not to be her tipple.

Too sweet, and she needed a clear head to ride her bike without lights.

"Now before either of you get any ideas about searching for George tonight, I want to tell you that we are not going to leave this house. If George wants to make a gesture like this, then I think we should allow him to do it."

"But Ma, he hates the dark."

"I know. That's why he took your lamp, and the torch. But maybe this will help him get over his fear. Darling, your father insisted that we stay here. Says I mustn't treat George like a baby, and he's right of course. With the supplies he took he's obviously planning an overnight sleep-out, probably in a friend's garden, or garage, something like that. We must let him do it without causing an uproar and embarrassing the poor little thing. The policeman was right, best let him come home of his own accord." She corked the bottle and looked at her watch. "Well, we won't have long to wait, will you look at the time? Now you do agree, don't you? We get a good night's sleep and be pleasant to George when he does come home. Mind you, I think your father plans to say a thing or two, but that's up to him."

Beatrice agreed and drifted off to bed. Rachel glared after her.

If you hadn't decided to marry your precious Joe, then Ma wouldn't have had the stupid dinner party, and poor George needn't've run away at all.

Suddenly she felt the strongest of dislikes for Beatrice, and wondered why she hadn't recognised the feeling sooner. Her mother watched, the bottle in her hand, then she took it back to the cupboard in the dining room, called "Good-night, dear" to Rachel, and went to bed.

Rachel took her father's point. If George wanted to make a gesture, then he should be allowed to make it, without his family going hysterical. But speaking for herself, the idea of going hysterical had strong appeal. So did the idea of going to look for George. But where to start was the problem, and how to carry out a proper search, and in or out of town? Should she just pedal up one street and down the next shouting "George, where are you?" Crashing into parked cars because she didn't have a lamp, and having non-parked cars crashing into her for the same reason?

Thanks to her mother's generous offering of the port, she had a queasy feeling in her stomach, and was wide-awake.

Maybe the quivering sadness she felt was owing to the port as well, but she thought not. So she took her overnight bag down from the top of her wardrobe and set it open on the bed. Then she began to pack into it all the odd bits and pieces that George had coveted from time to time, and that she had resolutely refused to part with. It was a strange collection. The big golden ball from Japan, that played "Hush-a-bye Baby" when you pulled its cord; a battered copy of *Dirty Beasts*, the waggish illustrations augmented over the years by crayons and coloured pencils; *Madeleine* with similar embellishments; and *The Catcher in the Rye;* a sloppy joe saying I'M A LOVER on the front, and OF RAIN FORESTS, on the back, far too big for him, but he'd wanted to borrow it for ages. Then she added her second-best pair of jeans, a bit tight for her, but the envy of George because of the number of zipped pockets, and her electric hairdryer as a bonus. She picked up the kaleidoscope, the possession that George envied her most, having broken his on its first day by trying to find out how it worked. She held it up to the light and the multitudinous slivers of glass danced and delighted her as they always had. She turned the cover a fraction, the colours frolicked as they changed places, then demurely settled down to await her applause. She put it back in its accustomed place and hid the bag underneath her bed.

Rachel thought of praying; was prepared to offer God anything at all in the way of promises if He would just keep George safe through the night, but as she had not considered herself to be on speaking terms with the Deity since her father had left it seemed somehow cheap to call upon Him now. So she sat on the bed and carefully folded the hem of the top sheet into fine and equally spaced pleats.

"All right, darling. I give up. Come and join us," her mother spoke from the door. "I've just found Beatrice reading the same page of a textbook for the fifteenth time, and I can't sleep, so we might as well clean up this mess in the kitchen."

Rachel had never heard housework sound so inviting, so they cleared away dishes, scraped, washed and dried, in a spirit more friendly than they had felt for some time. Rachel even managed to postpone allocating the blame for George's departure; poor Beatrice could hardly be blamed, she supposed, for being stupid enough to want to get married.

"Delicious meal, Ma," Beatrice murmured. "Sorry Joe's mother made such a fuss. Joe says she's never really settled down here."

"Well it's not surprising, is it dear? I mean Verona sounds so interesting. All of Italy sounds interesting. I suppose she misses her family, and Dante, and Veronese . . ."

Eh? What's got into you, Ma?

Both her daughters stopped in mid-wash-and-wipe to stare at their mother, who had obviously determined to look on the bright side of whatever problems were offered for consideration.

". . . You know, hearing them talk about Europe made me realise how little I know of the world. *I'd* like to travel, see Italy and France. Your father and I often talked about having a trip when you children were grown up."

"Arles sounds beautiful," Beatrice innocently offered.

"I would not be going to Arles," her mother said in stern and definite tones, and taking the vacuum cleaner from the cupboard she proceeded noisily and aggressively to clean the dining-room carpet.

After the chores were done they sat around the table in silence drinking coffee. As the darkness outside changed to a hazy blue, Beatrice turned off the light and opened the front door.

"He'll be back soon, Ma," she said, "don't worry. As soon as he gets hungry he'll come home."

"Of course he will." Her mother forced a weak smile. "I just bet you, if I put some bacon on to fry, George would come running in that door . . ." The smile was replaced by such a look of desolation that Rachel had to stand up and move away in case she began to bawl herself, loudly, like a little baby, which was what she so desperately wanted to do.

"Listen," she said instead, as she rinsed out their coffee mugs. "We're all tired, that's the problem. I feel a bit like I'm falling to pieces here myself. Why don't you have a nap, Ma, and as soon as he comes back we'll call you."

Her mother stood up and let Beatrice lead her from the room, but no sooner had they reached the hall than a car pulled up outside and their father stamped up the path. He was wearing the same suit he had worn the night before, and his eyes were bloodshot and strained.

"Not home yet, eh?" Rachel raced back to the kitchen to heat up coffee, surprised that her father hadn't already demanded it. "You know me, Janet, I am not a violent man. But when I find that young TOAD, there'll be hell to pay. And I hold you entirely responsible. Why didn't you tell me he was planning this?"

He was in the house by now, still stamping.

"Do sit down, Mac. You're making me much more nervous than I was already. How could I tell you when I didn't know myself? And what on earth have you been doing? You look as if you've been up all night."

And if you hadn't run off with Caroline, Ma wouldn't have put on the stupid dinner party and George wouldn't have had to run away. So I hold YOU entirely responsible for this, and I hope you HAVE been up all night.

"Here's coffee, Pa."

"As a matter of fact I have. Been up all night, driving around the place like a maniac looking for the little devil. Have you girls got any idea of where he might have gone?"

Now *his* face changed from anger to anguish and Rachel wondered if George could ever know how much they all loved him.

"Because if you do, tell me and I'll go there and belt the living daylights out of the little beggar. I swear I'll whack him until he's black and blue."

Rachel began to giggle, and thought she would never be able to stop, but the ringing of the telephone worked as effectively as a sharp slap across the face. She was closest, so she snatched it up before it was able to get into its stride. Paola Deladro was calling, and it seemed that her Guiseppe was missing too.

While Beatrice took over and spoke to her future mother-in-law Rachel decided that the reason why Mrs Deladro's English was hard to understand was that she actually pronounced every letter of every word. She practised doing it herself while her sister murmured comforting words into the phone and her parents stood together silently, shamelessly eavesdropping.

"Says he's been gone all night!" Beatrice whispered as she hung up. "Says he took her home and just drove off and didn't come back, and she doesn't know where he's gone, and she's all dressed and ready to go to Mass at Athelton. Boy, they certainly have their Masses early, don't they?"

She paused for a thoughtful moment, and Rachel could have sworn that she had stopped to weigh up the pros and cons of embracing Roman Catholicism. And made a quick decision against.

"Thing is, she seems to think he's with me, and how should I know where he's gone, and oh, Pa, where's he gone?"

Her father, looking worried, patted her gently on the back with one hand and stroked her hair with the other, and Rachel wished that Beatrice would just try to pull herself together for a change.

"Don't know, baby," he said. "But I tell you one thing. When that young swine of yours does turn up, I'm planning to belt the living daylights out of him too."

He raised reluctant smiles from all of them, but the smiles were tokens only.

"Come on," he urged, "what we all need is a square meal, that'll help us tackle the day's problems. Not that there'll be any problems of course. Those two boys are certain to turn up soon. I'm prepared to give them until midmorning, then I'll be on the rampage again to find them. Now what's on the menu for breakfast, Mother?"

It seemed almost like old times. Except that George was still missing, Beatrice's Joe had run away from home as well, and each one of them was beginning to doubt that things would ever be the same again.

11

Joe had not run away from home, of course. As the family was finishing breakfast his truck pulled in behind Mr Huntley's, and a radiant Beatrice ran outside to greet him.

"Well thank goodness, Joe's turned up."

Chooses a great time to drop in too. Doesn't he realise that we've got family problems here?

And of course Joe did know about the family problems, and had spent the night just as Mr Huntley had, driving around in a vain search for George.

And so he should, considering it's partly his fault.

"Come on, baby, cheer up." Her father smoothed down the hair on the top of her head, as he had been doing since she was a baby. The hair still grew in its own wilful, disorderly way and Rachel sometimes wondered if there was anything in the world that would discipline it, and longed for a wig. A whole shelf of wigs, in every colour imaginable. She snatched the opportunity to nuzzle against his shoulder, and felt ashamed of the way she was feeling about Joe, and about Beatrice, who had always been a reasonably tolerable sister she supposed, until now.

The Huntleys all waited in the kitchen while Joe telephoned his mother. The wrath of Paola was an emotion that none of them was eager to share. But he joined them afterwards with no signs of having suffered badly, and ate a hearty breakfast.

No one wanted to rest; no one wanted to stay at home waiting for George to come back; they all wanted to go and search for him. And while they were arguing about who should go, and whether it was necessary that anyone should wait at home, the doorbell rang. Rachel had been debating more forcefully than the rest, suspecting that she would be the one left at home to wait, so she did not hurry forward to see who had come. Her mother went and came back to the kitchen with, of all people, Miss Rose Follett, bearing a sizeable basket.

"Do forgive me for intruding. How do you do." Her wide smile included a startled Joe and Beatrice who had not seen her before. She was wearing a very long and voluminous dress sprigged with tiny blue roses, and a lavishly adorned straw hat that suggested picnics on the lawns of country houses, sedate games of croquet, and cucumber sandwiches. Or all of them at once, although there was a touch of eccentricity about the outfit that Rachel noticed but was unable to place.

"I saw you, Rachel, and you, Mr Huntley, at the cinema last night, with the torch. Don't suppose you noticed me, aisle seat, on the left, towards the back. I think that must be about the fifteenth time I've seen *The Maltese Falcon*. I enjoy it so much, but you know, I always have a secret hope that this time Mr Bogart might just find it in his heart to let her go free. Of course she was wicked, I know that . . .Oh I do apologise. I run on, don't I? I realised that you were seeking someone, but to my shame, I put it from my mind in my enjoyment of the film. But this morning at church, Mrs Wade — her husband is one of the local policemen — well you probably know that, but Mrs Wade happened to mention that your little boy had . . . er. Well,

I went back to the Walkers', I'm staying with them, old friend from schooldays, Margaret is, and I just thought I'd make up a few, well, you might find you can use, something to save you the chore of preparing a meal perhaps.''

She plonked the basket down on the table and paused to take a breath. Rachel, deciding that it might be considered piggish to peer inside, inhaled some very inviting odours, some sweet, some savoury. Then Miss Follett was away again.

"I know this is an intrusion, crashing in on you like this, hardly knowing you at all really. Well I have met you at the Craft Centre Mr Huntley, with Caro . . . and of course you, dear Rachel, but what I should like to suggest is that I do something to help. Now my friends do say that I am a help — sometimes — and I know how you must all be longing to be out looking for the little fellow, although I *am sure* he'll come running just as soon as he's hungry.''

Why does everyone insist on making poor George out to be such a glutton? He's a greedy little pig I do admit, but it's not for them to say.

"George is pretty good at looking after himself, Miss Follett, and he took plenty of stuff with him.''

Her mother interrupted, with an icy look to Rachel. "It was so kind of you to bring gifts of food, Miss Follett, I shan't have to bother about cooking now. But what else did you have in mind?''

"Oh, just a few scones, it's nothing, but do forgive me, I forgot to give you a message from the Walkers. Both send their love and they'll drop in later. Taking an old friend out for a drive today.'' Miss Follett looked ever so slightly shifty as she said that and Rachel wondered why. Both Walkers had been unreservedly friendly to all members of the family both before and after the split. Bede, of course, had maintained a steady course of being unreservedly *un*friendly. She supposed they felt guilty about not coming to help in the search at once, taking an old friend for a drive seemed a lame excuse. Her attention switched back on as the gangling visitor continued. "But I digress, now you were wondering how I could help, weren't you? Well I thought of manning the telephone, answering the door, taking messages, that sort of thing. Keeping things running smoothly here while you set about looking for him. You'll all feel better if you *do* something, I know."

Mac Huntley nodded. "Thank you, Miss Follett, I'm sure you're right. Joe, you and Beatrice search the south and west roads, and don't forget those back roads towards Athelton. Jan, you come with me and we'll go north and east. We report back here at one-thirty to attack Miss Follett's picnic."

"What about me, Pa? Who do I go with?"

Her father spoke very firmly and said, "You would help us all most, Rachel, by staying here to give Miss Follett a hand. If — when George comes home there should be a member of the family waiting I think."

Okay. So I'm being punished for snapping at stupid Miss Follett who should be at home minding her own business anyway.

There was no support to be had from her mother or Beatrice, and judging by the sly look on his face she suspected Joe of preparing another of his solicitous enquiries about her bad back, so she filled two flasks with hot coffee for them. Miss Follett brought forth from the basket scones and a date loaf studded with walnuts, so Rachel allocated food for each of the search-parties, and they were off.

Miss Follett carefully removed her wide hat and patted what could have been either a large apricot or a small pumpkin back into its place among the clusters of flowers and fruits.

"Lovely, isn't it?" she murmured, "Did the trimming myself. There's a little place I go to in the city where they sell every mortal thing you could imagine for trimming hats."

And you bought their entire stock for that one.

"They cater to the theatre trade mostly of course. But I like a hat that *celebrates* don't you?" And she placed the rejoicing object carefully on the sideboard. Rachel looked closer, and marvelled. There was a greenish rose, or was it a yellowing Brussels sprout? And there were bees, several of them, attached by fine nylon thread so that they bobbed about as the hat moved.

"Not real," Miss Follett assured her. "I could never bring myself to use living things as trimmings. Or *dead* living things either, of course, if you follow me. No, the little man at the shop makes those bees by hand for me. Why don't you try it on, dear. I'm sure it would suit your beautiful young face, and then you could borrow it if you like."

Rachel declined the offer. *If I did, sure as anything the doorbell'd ring at that exact instant, and I wouldn't be able to get the damn thing off probably, and I'd be stuck in it and a perfect stranger'd see me. Or worse, maybe Bede Walker!*

Instead she offered refreshments, wondering why all she could think of to do was eat and drink coffee. Miss Follett preferred tea, and chose not to have any of the food she had brought. Rachel decided that she would have none of it either, hoping that Miss Follett would notice and be chastened. So she took the big biscuit tin down from the dresser. It was a lot lighter than usual. She lifted the lid, and inside were some pieces of broken biscuit, and a large folded sheet of drawing paper.

On the paper, in bright purple crayon George had left a message.

Mon sher petty shoes, soyez tranquille. Je retourn domain matin. Toot sweet. Amour, George.

Rachel sat down quickly, the ache in her stomach and chest coming back as strongly as it had the evening before.

"He meant to come back this morning. How on earth did he manage to get the 'don't worry' right and all the rest so wrong? He *says* he'll be back this morning, and it's almost lunchtime, and to George morning means *morning*, I mean he's always first up. *Petty shoes!* And Miss Follett, if George says he'll do something then he *does* it. I mean he says this morning, and he even says *toot sweet!* Yikes, isn't his French terrible? But he said it, so something must have stopped him from coming home, because if George says . . ."

Miss Follett placed the mug of tea in Rachel's shaking hand and read the note herself.

"What an interesting boy," she said, "to write it in French. Or try to, anyway. But tell me dear, why on earth did he hide the note so carefully? And in a biscuit tin of all places?"

"He didn't hide it really. That biscuit tin is George's very favourite place. I mean he's *always* in there, practically lives in there, so he'd expect us to be in there quite a bit too, except that with the spiffy food last night, and all that stuff you brought, no one's bothered looking for a biscuit. Not that they'd have found one. He's only left a couple of broken ones, the little greedy-guts."

She could feel hot tears making her eyes itch, tears that would embarrass her to death at any other time. Today Miss Follett was standing quietly by, her long grey pigtail trailing down her bosom and tied with a green plastic sealer from a garbage-bag, her large hand patting Rachel's shoulder gently, without is customary clumsiness, and her calm dark eyes uncritical and again somehow forgiving, as they had been at the Craft Centre when Rachel had sharpened her talons on poor Bede — all bandages and plaster — years ago it seemed.

Rachel put her head down on the table and sobbed.

After a while Miss Follett fetched tissues. Neither said a word and just as Rachel had decided comfortably that no word need be said, the doorbell rang.

Rachel, sniffling, sensed who the visitor was even before she opened the door. He stood diffidently on the doormat, faded jeans too long, one leg folded back, the other concertina'd around his ankles, joggers so decrepit that grimy toes poked out through the top, and a T-shirt displaying a message unreadable now, because too many and varied meals had been carelessly eaten while the shirt was being worn. He smiled.

Wow! How do those teeth get to be so green?

"Hi, Whiffy."

"George come and play, cannee?"

"He's not home. You remember Whiffy, Dad and I asked you about it last night. *Only last night?* You said you hadn't seen him yesterday."

"No. Not to speak to. I dint."

Whiffy was troubled, he obviously had something on his mind, so Rachel took him through to the kitchen, standing as far back as decency allowed. Miss Follett didn't seem to notice a thing. She poured him a glass of milk and buttered a scone which he removed from sight as efficiently as George ever had. Then she offered cake and they sat opposite while he took that a little more slowly. The eating seemed to relax him.

"Whiffy," Rachel said in a quiet conversational tone, "When was the last time you saw George. To talk to."

Whiffy stared as he rammed the last chunk of cake into his mouth with an open hand. Then he drank the rest of the milk and carefully licked off the resulting moustache.

Whiffy Baker, answer me now or I total you. And that's a solemn promise.

"Friday. I see 'im Friday, to talk to. I gotta go now." He pushed back the chair and would have scuttled away, but Miss Follett leaned across the table and murmured.

"You are George's best friend I think, dear, and he yours?"

"S'right." He lingered, but still prepared for flight.

"Well we have a problem, you see, and I'm almost certain that you are the only person in the world who can help us because you two are such close friends. You see, George promised to come home this morning, and he's not here. So something must have prevented him from coming. Do you agree?"

Whiffy nodded, and Rachel silently applauded Miss Follett's superior interrogation methods.

"Will you tell us what you and George did on Friday, er, Whiffy? You're the only one who knows, you see, and we think it might help if we know too. Help George, I mean."

Whiffy weakened. He and George had gone off on their bicycles on Friday, yabbying. "Fishing for yabbies," he kindly elaborated for an intrigued Miss Follett. "You got this bit of meat see, and you tie it on this bit of string. And what you do is you let it down in the water in the dam and them yabbies they grab a hold and you haul 'em up and get 'em off quick so's you save your meat for the next time, see."

"A sort of crayfish, I gather," Miss Follett nodded. "And do you eat them?"

And are we wasting time here?

"Nah. We throw 'em back in, so's they'll be there when we come back the next time, see."

Miss Follett appeared relieved at this sporting attitude. "And what did you and George do then, Whiffy?"

Whiffy was reluctant to answer at first, but she persisted, assuring him that any secrets were safe with her, and also with Rachel, but should be told because George might be in terrible danger.

So poor loyal little Whiffy, sweating and scratching, told them the secret that he had promised his friend he would keep for his entire life no matter what. The secret that was supposed to go with him to the grave, even if they pulled his fingernails out one by one and lit fires in his ears. He and George had taken a solemn oath on it, and now here he was, telling Rachel and the tall scraggy weird-looking woman, because with her looking at him like that it seemed he had no choice at all.

But he had a comfortable feeling that it was all right to tell, that George would approve. And he didn't even seem to be sweating as much as he usually did.

That was a comfortable feeling too.

12

The family was due back, so there was no sense in setting out themselves, although Rachel was longing to be the first to find George. The three of them sat in relaxed silence around the table and before very long they heard a car pull in to the drive.

Miss Follett put a restraining hand on Whiffy's arm and Rachel dashed out through the back door and around the corner of the house.

"He's probably at a place called Summering," she shouted, and wondered why her mother and father froze getting out of the car, as if they were playing a crazy game of statues. Then her mother turned her head to look across the top of the car at her husband.

"Summering," she said in a surprisingly normal tone of voice considering the look of venom on her face. "What would my son be doing at Summering?"

Mac Huntley moved at last and walked around the car to stand in front of Rachel. "What about Summering?" he said.

So Rachel took them inside, and Whiffy, standing confidently now beside Miss Follett, told them about the yabbying, and then he told them about the secret place that he and George had found, that nobody else in the whole entire universe was supposed to know about. The place that he reckoned old George might have gone to when he decided to run away from home.

"I'da gone out there this morning, looked meself, if I'da thought about it. Din't think about it, until she asked me." He nodded towards Miss Follett, who swung her plait in a self-conscious way and shrugged.

Janet turned again to her husband, and in the same quiet conversational tone that she had used by the car said, "You know about this place?"

He nodded. "I'll go now."

"No," she said loudly. "I'm coming with you. Rachel, you stay here and tell the others."

It did not seem to be an appropriate time to suggest lunch, nor did Rachel feel that a protest would be successful, but no sooner had they gone than Beatrice and Joe arrived back.

"Hey," Joe said as he snatched a slice of date loaf to go on with. "You girls want to be in on this. Let's all go and find the kid together, eh?"

So they set off again, Beatrice and Joe in the runabout truck, with a grinning Whiffy, the famous solver of the mystery, standing proudly on the back with his face defying the wind. Miss Follett offered to take Rachel in her small Volkswagen, and they sped along behind the others with Whiffy indicating turns for them in a very bossy fashion as they headed out of town along the road to Bindah. After a while they took the left fork and the road became a track, rutted and stony, with the hill on one side, and a gully on the other. They turned off this on to an even narrower trail, and then they came to a fence, and a broken-down gate, left open for so long that its base was lost among weeds.

With Whiffy waving them to follow, they drove

through, and as they did Rachel noticed a battered sign, pitted with bullet holes, flapping sadly from the centre of the gate.

On it was painted in faded letters, SUMMERING.

Away to their left on a slight rise stood a large pile of blackened stones, and what remained of three chimneys. There were trees there, and signs of hedges and a garden. But Whiffy directed them to the right across the dry paddock, to bump and lurch along a track that was hardly defined at all. They rounded a cluster of gum trees and came upon the dam where Whiffy and George did their yabbying. It was half full of muddy water and they did not stop, because across the far side of the paddock they could see Mac Huntley's car parked beside an enormous old pepper tree. Miss Follett parked the Beetle behind Joe's truck and they hurried together towards the tree.

Whiffy lifted a low-hanging bough and a wide doorway of fronds swung aside to allow them to walk, stooped a little, into the great cavern under the tree's leafy skirts. It was cool in there, with a pungent peppery smell and a dirt floor that seemed to have been swept clean.

In the middle of the area, beside the huge bole of the tree, a small hut had been built. There was a narrow doorway with a length of hessian (an old wheat-bag slit to size), nailed to the top to serve as a door. There was a small window with a wooden shutter tied back with fencing wire. The walls were made of old kerosene tins cut open and hammered flat and nailed to a few roughly trimmed logs, and it was roofed with rusty off-cuts of corrugated iron.

In front of the little house there was a low seat made of two tree-stumps with a plank laid across them. On this seat Mr and Mrs Huntley were sitting. He was holding her close and she was crying and neither looked up at the new arrivals.

Rachel had never seen her parents so distraught, not

even at the time of their separation. The others hung back, but she walked slowly forward, pulled aside the rough cloth of the door and peered into the hut. The whole area measured no more than two metres by one and a half. Some ragged velvet cushions were stacked in one corner, an old meat-safe stood in another, a folding card-table with its legs cut off short leaned against the back wall which was in fact the trunk of the tree, and George's unrolled sleeping-bag lay in the middle of the dirt floor.

She stepped across it and opened the wire-mesh door of the meat-safe. On one shelf was a pile of yellowed MAD magazines and a box of playing-cards. On another was a biscuit tin containing a very meagre selection of broken biscuits, a tin of sardines and a large Coke bottle half full of water. And on the third shelf in a guilty group stood a plastic tobacco-pouch, a packet of cigarette papers, and a box of matches.

Whiffy came through the doorway behind her. "This is private property y'know. We don't let people come here." But it was a half-hearted rebuke. The important thing was that George was not there, and there was no sign that he had spent the night there either.

"Never mind, Whiff. It's okay." Rachel steered him back outside and was glad to see that her parents were now on their feet and ready to leave.

"Police station," her father said, "we'll have to get them moving now. He's come here to leave the sleeping-bag and then he's gone off again. Come along, Janet." They left together, each looking sadly frail.

The others followed and as they drove past the burned-out ruin of the homestead on the hill Rachel wondered who had lived there, what had happened to them, and which of their children had built the little cubbyhouse under the pepper tree.

"Shan't talk if you'd rather not," Miss Follett hiccupped as the little car jolted over the stones to the gate. "I can be quiet, although you might not think so to hear me running on at times. I tend to be nervous with new people, you know."

I know. Like you were at our place this morning.

"Are you really? You're a famous artist, you should be confident."

"Me? A famous artist? That's my friend Margaret Walker been exaggerating again. She's very kind, but I'm not even a good artist I'm afraid, let alone famous. Oh I teach, and I think I am a competent teacher, because I can see when they get it right, although I can't seem to get it right myself. Funny, isn't it?"

Rachel agreed, remembering the eccentric sign at the Craft Centre, and Miss Follett went on.

"The thing that I excel at is, I think, enthusiasm. I really enjoy doing things, and my girls at school seem to catch a little of that you know. I hope they do anyway. But that's enough about me. Famous artist! How silly! I like this town, you know Rachel. This is my first visit and you've all been so friendly to me."

"I haven't been very friendly. Sorry."

Miss Follett risked a nasty accident by turning her head to smile at her passenger.

"You're a dear girl, and you're going through a very trying time." She was silent then, all the way to the police station.

It was the same policeman on duty that Rachel and her father had met the previous night, Sergeant Wade, Rachel presumed, spouse of the churchgoing and chatty Mrs Wade. He was much more willing to help them now, but more harassed than he had been. It seemed the patrol car had been busier than usual during the night. Still was busy in fact, checking out stories of motorbike gangs raging along the roads around town. When he heard this, Joe, who had been at the forefront of the group, stepped back and began very carefully to study a roster list that was pinned to the noticeboard on the far wall.

"Noisy beggars," the sergeant went on, "burning up and down the roads since before daylight. It's them Eyeties from out Athelton way. Hundreds of 'em, got these gangs, see. Don't give us much trouble in the normal way of things, but they must be having one of them meetings this weekend, races and that. We got reports from all over the district, people see them going by, in twos and threes mostly, just to put us off the track see, but by the time the patrol car gets there they're off somewhere else, aren't they? Now this lad of yours, when was the last time you saw him?"

Rachel remembered coming back from her visit to the Craft Centre on Friday afternoon, talking to him about joining forces in a business venture and being scorned, leaning against the veranda post near the kitchen door. And she remembered George asking if he could borrow her bicycle lamp. She tried to recall the actual moment that she had put her bike back in the storeroom, to see if George's sleeping-bag was on the shelf then. It seemed to her that it was not, and George had been out with his bike when she set off for the Craft Centre, therefore it was probable that he'd pedalled out to the hut on Friday to leave the sleeping-bag, meaning to return with only the rucksack on Saturday.

"Lunch on Saturday. He was at home for lunch on Saturday," her mother said. "Remember girls, I'd been to the hairdresser's and he said . . . he admired my hair and we all laughed at him because he . . . he said it in French, and he didn't get it right. He said, *mon cher maman*, which is masculine of course, and then he told me that my horses were pretty. And we laughed at him. And I can't recall seeing him after that."

"I did," Beatrice remembered. "I told him about five o'clock to go and have a shower so that he'd be ready in time for the party. He was rummaging in the biscuit tin when I saw him, and I told him not to be such a little glutton, to save some of his appetite for dinner. And that was the last time I saw him." Both she and her mother showed signs of approaching sobs, so Mr Huntley gave a nod to Miss Follett, who gently ushered them across to chairs and sat them down.

Just then the phone on Sergeant Wade's desk rang and he snatched it up, and muttered into the mouthpiece while the Huntleys and Joe eagerly listened in.

It was not news of George. It was the police at Athelton ringing to say that one of the motorcycles that had been rampaging around the district had been involved in an accident. The driver, one of the young Italians from a farm nearby, had escaped unhurt, but his injured pillion passenger was being taken to the local hospital.

"You won't believe this, Charley," the voice on the telephone squeaked, "but it was a woman. Good-looker too, red hair. Lad claims she's his auntie. Beats me what they'll be up to next."

All eyes turned to Joe, who grabbed Beatrice by the arm and crashed out of the office. They listened as the truck started up and roared off down the street. Then they turned back to the desk to plan their search for George.

13

It was dark by the time Miss Follett and Rachel pulled up outside the Walkers' house. Miss Follett had a key to let them in, and yoo-hooing loudly, she led the way down the hall to the sunroom at the back of the house.

Bede Walker lounged on the sofa, his broken leg propped up on the armrest. Beside him sat the beautiful Sandra, in pink jeans today, and a fluffy pink sweater. Bede's good arm was draped across her shoulders.

If those pants were any tighter you'd be arrested, Sandra my girl.

"Hi, Sandra. Hi, Bede."

It took them a moment to realise that there was someone else in the room, because Bede was plugged in to the earphones of the radio, and Sandra's technicolour eyes were fixed on the television screen. When they did click back into the present Bede explained that he had been instructed by his father to listen with care to the local radio station, in case any reports were broadcast of a small boy being found. Sandra had volunteered to help by monitoring the television, but since she happened to be watching a city station showing a football match, Rachel thought it extremely unlikely that Sandra would be of any help at all.

"The Olds aren't home yet, Miss Follett. You got any news?" But he could tell by their expressions that they had no news, and he slid his hand back from Sandra's neck, and even made a clumsy attempt to stand up.

Don't stop on my account, please. Do grope on. It doesn't bother me *at all.*

"Not yet, dear. Your parents are still out searching with dear Caroline of course."

"But Miss Follett, you said they were taking an old friend for a drive." Rachel had the feeling that too many things were going on behind her back.

"Well, Caroline is an old friend, dear. She and Mr Walker grew up together. Didn't you know that?"

Rachel had the feeling that *far* too many things were going on behind her back, and that they were making her feel extremely bewildered. But she had no time to question Miss Follett any further because they had torches to collect, and blankets in case they found George injured, a first-aid kit for the same reason, and there was a lengthy note to be left for the Walkers. Sandra teetered into the kitchen and made them a big flask of coffee in an irritatingly efficient way, and Rachel decided that from that day on the act of drinking coffee would always give her heartburn. Acute heartburn.

As they were leaving, Rachel was somewhat disgruntled to see that Bede and Sandra were settling down in their previous positions, she staring intently again at the screen, he with his arm on her shoulder. Some people didn't seem to care very much about some other people's problems, she reflected. That good foot tempted her, but she fought down the urge to put it out of action, and followed Miss Follett to the car.

They had been given specific directions, and were to search roads to the south. As they drove through town, Rachel was astonished to see so many cars, and station wagons, and trucks, and bicycles, and vans, all out on the street on what would normally be a quiet Sunday evening.

"Aren't people admirable," Miss Follett commented. "The word has gone around, you see. That was the Reverend Parker's car we just passed. He's probably sent the whole congregation out to look for your brother. And no doubt Father Ryan has done the same. Your family has a lot of friends in this town, Rachel."

"Speaking of friends, Miss Follett. I didn't know that Mr Walker and Caroline were old friends. Caroline only came here about four months ago." The silence had to be bridged. "Didn't she?"

Miss Follett was flustered and fiddled with the gears and turned the windscreen wipers on, although it was a clear night. "Well dear," she finally offered, "from what I've heard, and believe me, I haven't been listening to gossip, it's just what I've heard, being an old friend of Margaret Walker. Caroline lived here when she was a child, until she was grown-up in fact. And then she went away. And came back, as you said, about four months ago. And that's absolutely all I know. So there's no use your asking me anything about it at all. Really there isn't."

"About what?"

"About anything. About any possible thing in the world. There's no use asking *me*. Now get the torch out ready, dear, we have to search the roadside from here."

The theory was that George had been riding along one of the roads leading out of town, and had been knocked off his bicycle, so they were seeking wheel tracks in the gravel at the side of the road, a bicycle in the ditch, and an injured George. Rachel knew that a hit-and-run accident was unlikely to have remained undiscovered for so long, and she suspected that she was not the only person dreading worse fates for her brother.

"I've an idea." Miss Follett stopped the car. "Now

what do you think of this? We leave the car here, take the torches, and walk along the side of the road. Can't hope to see any tracks as we drive. Oh look, there's someone coming in the other direction doing just that.'' So they left the car and walked along the edge of the road shining their torches into the ditch, exchanging unsmiling and anxious waves with the other group of searchers who passed them. When they arrived at the spot where the next car was parked they turned back, and thus drove, parked, and plodded on through the evening, with their hopes lessening as the darkness thickened.

"He won't be along this road, anyway," Rachel moaned. "It's exactly opposite the road to Bindah, and he'd have to take that one to get back to, what's the name of the place?"

"I don't know, dear. I know absolutely nothing. Nothing. About anything at all. Now what about another cup of coffee?"

"I've got palpitations already from drinking so much coffee. It's not good for you, you know. In fact, I don't think I ever want to see another cup of coffee in my entire life. Thank you very much. And the name of the place is Summering."

The night dragged on, broken by the frequent headlights of cars driven slowly, seeking turn-offs that had to be investigated. Drivers shouted news of no news, offered hopeful wishes, and with each one that passed Rachel was convinced that her brother would never be found alive.

But he was.

It was after midnight, and they were a long long way from town, when they heard the noise of a continuously tooting motorcycle horn in the distance. It came closer, stridently shattering the night into pieces, and they could see its light sending wavering beams into the dark as the driver rode it unsteadily and fast over the corrugations. Then they heard the voice, a very loud male voice shouting with jubilation words they could not yet make out.

"Well, bless my soul," Miss Follett murmured. "Sounds like one of those marvellous cantors, doesn't he? Or a muezzin."

Rachel decided not to ask for a translation at that moment. She might have time some day to check the words in the big encyclopaedia. Whoever the voice belonged to, cantor or moo-whatever, it sounded great.

The voice and the motorbike came closer. Rachel dashed into the centre of the road, waving her torch up and down. The voice was very loud now, chanting in time to the bleat of the horn.

"They found him! They found him! They found him!"

The bike skidded to a stop beside her, a pair of leather-clad arms tossed a helmet from shaggy hair and grabbed her, and a hairy face chafed hers.

"You Rachel?"

Imprisoned as she was, and sobbing with relief, all she could manage was a sniffling nod.

"Well, Joe said I was to find you. You specially. Tell you they found him. Tell you he's alive."

Miss Follett and the searchers from the other side of the road were more able to speak, and they asked the questions for her. The hairy man kept his arms around her, for which Rachel was thankful, knowing she was bound to fall to the ground in a dead faint should he let go, and he told them as much as he knew.

His father had a spotlight on his truck, handy on the farm for spotting kangaroos in the culling season. He had been out on his bike all day (and all night, Rachel suspected, one of the bikie gang the policeman had complained of, no doubt). So when it began to get dark his father got out the old vehicle and went to the road where logically George would be found. The road to Bindah. And Summering.

The road was thronged with searchers, but his father's light was stronger than even the police car's, and at last it picked out a tiny reflection from the bicycle way down in the gully.

"Wouldn't spot it in daylight, probably," he told them. "There were bushes all around it, only a bit of metal showing. And the poor little kid was a long way from the bike they say. Only found him when they climbed down."

"You mean to tell me that we've all driven along that road twice today and he was lying there all the time and we didn't even notice *anything?*"

Her tone was so accusatory that the poor rider quickly took his arms away and reached for his helmet. To hide inside.

"Nobody did. Notice anything. It was Pop's searchlight that picked up just a little glint of metal down there. Can't blame anyone for not finding him earlier."

The other searchers were full of delight but very glad to be able to give up and go home. The ones closest were a young married couple, Rachel knew the man, he was a gardener in the main park, and his wife confided that they had left their two small children in the care of their grannie. Her eyesight was bad, so she had volunteered to stay at home, and the poor wife knew that both the children would already be showing the first signs of dental caries because of the rich food the old lady would have been plying them with, to say nothing of the threat to their personalities from watching a night of violence on television.

"She spoils them rotten you know, but she means well I suppose," she whispered. "Trouble is, I can't say anything, see, 'cause she's *his* mum.'' This with a toss of her head towards her quiet and obedient husband. Rachel felt a tinge of pity for him, and also for his poor mum who was home making whoopee with her grandchildren. A whoopee that was rare and punishable by the sound of things. But she was touched by the kindness they had shown by coming out in the night, and she thanked them sincerely, then turned to question the young man.

"Just how badly is he hurt?" she enquired.

He put the helmet right on then, and pushed the visor up so that he could talk.

"I don't know. They were putting him into the ambulance when I got there, and Joe wouldn't let me stay. Made me turn right around and find you."

He was hedging, Rachel could tell.

"You said he was alive. Well how alive was he? He's been out there for ages. Was he conscious at least?"

He turned his bike and threw his leg over the seat.

"No. He wasn't conscious. He'd been lying there for a day and a night remember. All last night and all today. I reckon you'd better prepare yourself for the fact that he's probably pretty badly hurt. But I don't know any more. And I've got to get back to the hospital myself."

"Why? Are you hurt?"

"Nope. It's my aunt. Stupid female fell off my bike this morning. She's in there with a broken leg."

Blimey! I bet she's giving the nurses hell. And this must be one of the cousins!

14

They squealed into the hospital car park and Miss Follett eased her little Beetle into a vacant spot behind Mac Huntley's car.

"I'll be pushing off soon anyway dear. Don't want to intrude, but I would like to know how the little one is. If nobody minds."

Rachel assured her that no one would mind and had a strong urge to beg her to stay. Somehow life seemed much easier to cope with when Miss Follett was around. They went in through the Emergency section and were directed upstairs. It was quiet and gloomy in the corridors, with small night-lights down at floor level, the purring sound of machinery, and the swish of nurses' uniforms as they padded about quietly between the wards. They ascended in the big, trolley-sized lift, and tiptoed along to the sisters' station, a glassed-in cubicle with a reading lamp focused low on the desk, and a panel of button lights beside it. As Rachel watched one of the lights glowed red, and a quiet buzzer sounded.

There was a plump sister at the desk, and she stood up as they approached and nodded her head towards the red button and rolled her eyes.

"Fourth time in the last hour," she said. "That Mr Brown sure likes to get his money's worth. You're the little boy's sister, aren't you? Along here."

"How is he?"

"Nothing wrong with the old devil. Goes home tomorrow. Oh, you mean your brother? Sorry. You'll have to ask the doctors, love. In there."

She waved at a door for them to enter, and hurried off on squeaky rubber soles to succour Mr Brown.

By the way the sister had spoken, Rachel had expected to find a panel of doctors sitting beyond the door. Instead she found it to be a sparse waiting room. Her parents and Beatrice and Joe were there, sitting in low chairs with a coffee table in the middle. On the table was a box of tissues, four abandoned paper cups containing dregs of a rusty-coloured liquid, and an ailing pot-plant.

Her mother had a black eye, and Rachel made a mental note to ask how she'd got it, later on.

George was in the operating theatre. Joe and Beatrice had seen him when he was found. He had been unconscious and covered in blood, but the ambulance driver had told them that blood didn't mean anything, it was what was there after the blood had been cleaned away that was important. They relayed this message to Rachel who didn't believe it. Any blood on poor little George meant trouble. They also told her that the doctor would come when they finished fixing George up, to tell them how badly he had been hurt.

A very deep melancholy settled on Rachel then. An awareness that there was absolutely nothing she could physically do to help her own brother, that it depended entirely on some unknown doctors' skills whether or not he would survive. She wondered if the others were as sure as she was that George had been gravely injured, and hoped not. She could probably manage to cope with things herself but it was better that her mother, for one, didn't worry too much.

Miss Follett gave her a quick hug. "I'll be on my way now, dear." She turned to Janet and Mac Huntley. "I am so joyful that your son has been found. I am available to help in any way I can, please remember that. And may I tell the Walkers? They probably know by now, of course, the news does get around fast, doesn't it? Good and bad. It's just that I am staying with them, and they have been out, looking for him. With Caroline of course."

An astonishing thing happened then.

Rachel's mother raised her hand and said, "Please, could you wait? Just for a moment." Then she sat very still, staring with her one good eye, straight ahead but *at* nothing. Apart from being battered about the left eye she looked so ineffably sad that everyone in the room seemed to be affected, the nature of the silence changed, and Rachel wanted desperately to go across and offer some comfort. She moved slightly and the pressure from Miss Follett's hand on her shoulder increased, strongly, so she settled back to wait with the others until her mother's decision was made.

Then Mrs Huntley stood up, dabbed at her black eye and walked across to where her husband was slouched, exhausted, in the other chair. He seemed to be asleep, but Rachel knew he wasn't, because he had nodded, and half risen when she and Miss Follett had come into the room.

She touched him gently on the shoulder.

"Mac," she said, "I think we should ask Miss Follett to tell Caroline to come. You may need her with you."

Mac opened his eyes, and Rachel wished he would close them again, so that the pain might stay hidden.

"Are you quite sure?" he muttered.

She nodded and came across to the door. "Please ask

Caroline if she would come, Miss Follett. We should like her to be here with us."

Miss Follett nodded and left the room, and Rachel realised that the whole family did share her despairing fears about George. Beatrice's hand was clasped like a claw over Joe's arm, and her lovely face was blotchy and red-eyed, while Joe himself was tense and haggard.

She sat down on the edge of the nearest chair and clenched her hands between her knees. The carpet had tiny orange blobs on it, orange for keeping people cheerful, she supposed, so she began to count all the blobs that were in the space under the coffee-table legs. It was impossible to do, because the blobs blurred together after a few moments. So she blinked and tried again by counting two sides and multiplying them, but for some reason she couldn't manage to keep the figures steady in her head for long enough to finish the job. And she was good at maths at school.

"Thanks for sending that guy out to tell me, Joe." It seemed necessary to keep the voice low, and she had to say it twice before Joe focused his eyes on her and understood.

He nodded. "That's okay, Rachel."

She wondered if it would upset him too much, then decided that manners insisted that she ask, so she whispered again, "How's your mother?"

"Fracture. Leg. Some bruises. Lucky she was wearing a helmet." It was Beatrice who answered. "They're keeping her in for a while for tests in case she's got internal injuries. Joe feels bad because he didn't fetch her this morning, you know, when she rang about going to Mass."

This morning! That was years ago!

"As soon as she hung up the telephone they said she rushed out and caught Ricco as he came up to the house to collect a map. She grabbed a spare helmet as she went and didn't even wait to change out of her church clothes.

Hitched up her skirt and nipped on to the pillion and poor old Ricco had to take her with him, and he hadn't even tried riding with a passenger before."

She was rattling on, almost hysterical, and Joe patted her hand. "Take some deep breaths, baby," he said. "I should have gone out and fetched her. She said she wanted to help, but, you know, I didn't realise how much. But anyway, they'd just made it to the main road and old Ricco hit a bump and off she flew. Well they both did, but Rick wasn't hurt, and of course one of the nosy neighbours'd been carrying on about the noise of the bikes, and he was watching, good thing really, because he called the ambulance and they brought her in here. You meet a guy with a camera when you came in?"

"No. Thousands of cars in the car park, though, and some people standing around. Who's the guy with the camera?"

"Reporter from the local rag. They're all out there, him, and the radio roundsman, someone said a television van was on its way too. George is big news you know."

Rachel thought how George would have loved it. Interviews, fame, star of stage, screen and radio, television contracts for leading roles in soapies, all would have been meat and drink for George. And he was in the operating theatre.

She breathed deeply and steadily. For George as well as for herself.

What question do I dare ask first? Why does Ma want Caroline to come here? Why was she so upset today when I mentioned Summering? And how in hell did she come by that shiner?

"How old is he?"

Beatrice looked alarmed. "He's twelve, Rach. George is twelve. Birthday in April. Are you all right?"

"Of course I know how old George is. I was thinking of the other one. That Ricco. Only because I wondered if he was old enough to ride a motorcycle. Don't they have to have licences?"

Joe turned on her angrily. "Of course he's got a licence. He's my cousin, Uncle Angelo's son. One of the 'Eyeties' that cop was talking about. Bikie gangs! Huh. There's only eight of them got bikes, maybe nine, and they're not a bikie gang, use them on the farms mainly."

"I only asked . . ."

"Right. And I'm telling you. He's eighteen years old, finishes school at Athelton end of this year. Good student. Top footballer. Name's Rossi, Riccardo Rossi, and Rossi means red, to save you looking it up. Okay?"

All this had been hissed, and as both the senior Huntleys had their eyes closed, pretending to be asleep, they tactfully kept them that way. Beatrice did not move, undecided which loyalty she should follow. And Rachel went back to counting the blobs on the carpet. Deeply ashamed, and not of any one thing in particular, just ashamed.

"Hey, Rachel. I'm sorry." Joe spoke more loudly this time, and Rachel looked up. The arm that Beatrice was attached to was not available for use of course, and he was unable to stand up without disturbing her, but he stretched out the other hand towards Rachel, and unsmiling said, "I really do apologise."

He made no excuses, didn't say "we're all upset", and things like that that people often say to justify bad behaviour. Even more likely to win Rachel's approval was the fact that he didn't say, "will you forgive me?" a tricky device that blackmailed the forgiver sometimes before she was ready to forgive, and left her feeling worse than the forgivee.

So Rachel stretched her hand out too, and clasped his and said, "That's okay, Joe. Reckon we could be square now?"

Joe nodded and smiled and suddenly Rachel could

understand why Beatrice loved him. She resumed her tally of the carpet blobs, and wondered if her parents were praying, and whether she should try to pray now as well, or whether God might consider it an impertinence after all this time.

Before she could make the decision the door opened and a middle-aged man came in. He was wearing a wrinkled blue gown, a blue cotton cap, and big blue cotton bootees. Rachel recognised him as the surgeon who had taken her appendix out the year before, and her parents knew him well. She was glad he'd been with George.

All four of them stood up, and Rachel for one held her breath.

"He's alive. Very badly injured I'm afraid, Janet, Mac." He nodded towards the others as if he really couldn't spare the time to name them as well, but he was aware that they were there, and interested. "But he's a sturdy little bloke. Strong heart."

Just then the door swung open again and Caroline came into the room. She walked past the doctor and stood silently beside Mac Huntley.

"Caroline." The surgeon acknowledged her as if she too was an old friend. "We've done all we can at the moment. He's taken it very well so far."

"What about sending him to the city? For better equipment? I'll charter a plane. Could you come along, Bill?"

"Hey, Mac, slow down. The lad's too fragile to move at the moment."

Caroline spoke. "What about flying a second opinion up?" She leaned across Mac. "What do you think, Janet?"

The doctor answered first. "I'm all for it, in fact I was about to suggest it. I know a man brilliant in this area."

Just what does he mean, "this area"?

Janet Huntley spoke up. "Yes. I want as many opinions and as much help as we can get. Anything."

"Good. I'll put in a call right away. He starts early."

Rachel looked towards the windows and saw that it was day.

Which area? For God's sake ask him someone!

Her mother spoke again. "Just what sort of injuries has he, Bill? Please, we'd rather you told us everything you've found so far. I think we'd all prefer to know how bad he is, wouldn't we? So that we know what we have to face."

Her special look was for Rachel, the other one in the room who had no one to lean on. Rachel swallowed and lifted her head in preparation for the blow, then nodded her readiness to accept it.

Dr Jarvis fiddled with the tapes of his silly little blue cap, and took it off. He shook his head wearily, then *he* swallowed and lifted *his* head. And told them what injuries George had suffered on Saturday night on the road to Summering.

15

Rachel hauled the overnight bag out from under her bed. She unzipped it and made a narrow nest between the sloppy joe and the jeans. Without holding it up to her eye, without giving the tube even a single rotation she took the kaleidoscope from the bookcase and laid it gently in the space. Then she closed the bag and put it down near the door.

She lay on the bed, not expecting to sleep, and was startled when she woke to find that five hours had passed; it was mid-afternoon and no one else was at home. She found a note on the kitchen table — one of her mother's cryptic attempts to frustrate burglars — with HOS.2 B,I.L,M. scrawled on it, so she had a quick shower, a slice of Miss Follett's bacon-and-egg pie, and a glass of milk. Then she dressed and dragged her bicycle out of the storeroom, not looking at the empty spaces left by George's bike and the sleeping-bag and the rucksack.

As she came around the side of the house wheeling the bike, Joe's truck pulled up at the gate and Beatrice and Joe walked up the path.

"Still unconscious, but he's hanging in there," Beatrice said. "The guy from the city operated as soon as he flew in, and they say the operation was a success, but that only means that he's still alive. They won't really know anything until he's conscious again."

"Ma left a note to say that you and she went to the hospital at two o'clock. I'm on my way."

"Well she says would you wait until she comes home, and you can go with her tonight. Make us a cup of coffee will you, love?"

"You've inherited that from Pa you know, Bea. 'Make us a cup of coffee will you, love?' Next thing you'll drop everything to write The Great Australian Novel, so watch it. They okay?"

Beatrice nodded and sat wearily at the kitchen table while Rachel boiled the water and ground the beans. "Pa's the hardest hit. Just sits there. You know I think he feels it's all his fault."

He's got a point there. If he hadn't left us, George wouldn't have had to run away.

"Maybe some of it is."

Joe got the cups down and carried them over to the table. "That's crazy. Not his fault George came off his bike."

"Well, if he hadn't left us . . ."

"Listen, Rach, sure poor old George was upset. You were all upset, but how far back do you go to allocate the blame here? I mean if your dad hadn't run off with Caroline, if your mother hadn't married him, if *their* parents hadn't had them in the first place. You could go back yonks, trying to blame someone. Doesn't get you anywhere. The facts are that George went off on his bike about dusk when the light's not good. I reckon that damn bike's too big for him anyway, probably wobbling along with the weight of that blasted rucksack, hit a stone at the wrong part of the road and just kept going over and over until he came to the bottom of the gully. The weight of the rucksack was enough to keep the poor little beggar tumbling. But do you blame the bloke whose car hit that stone one day and tossed it on to that exact spot on the road? Is it his fault? The surveyor who put the road there, right beside that gully?"

"Okay. It's no one's fault. How did Ma get that black eye?"

She thought they might never manage to tell her because they laughed so much. But between them they gasped it out.

When George was found his parents were back at the police station, giving a fuller description of George and some photographs to the sergeant. Also at the police station was the young reporter from the local paper, complete with notebook and a cluster of photographic equipment.

"You know little Charlie Sutcliff, Rach? Talk about Mr Big-deal! Apparently he had all these cameras and flashes and things slung around his neck, and he was badgering the policeman for a scoop . . ."

"Scoop Sutcliff! Don't, you're killing me!"

"Anyway, back at the scene of the accident, as they say on the best news broadcasts, as soon as Uncle Angelo's beam hit George's bike, my cousin Gina hit the road. She'd gone with him as lookout. You'd like her, Rach, about your age, she's a great little sprinter. Well Gina hooted off to find the police car that'd been cruising up and down that road because they figured he'd most likely be found there, and they send off a radio message to town . . ."

"Anyway, as soon as the message came through young Scoop started throwing his weight around, asking fool questions, like 'How do you feel now that your son's been found, Mrs Huntley?' Things like that. Well you can imagine how Ma and Pa reacted."

"You mean *Pa* socked Ma in the eye?"

"No, stupid, they just barged out to the car to scream off to the Bindah road . . ."

"But our intrepid reporter doesn't have a car you see, so he leapt in beside your mother and they just didn't have time to turf him out, so he travelled out there with them . . ."

"No doubt asking deep and meaningful questions all the way!"

"They arrived just as the ambulance men were bringing George back up. We were there by then, and of course your parents wanted to get as near as they could, and this yahoo kept flashing his camera and badgering them . . ."

"So Ma hauled off and socked him!"

"She never!"

"She did! She just sized him up, planted her feet, spat on her fist, and let him have it."

"Laid him out cold."

"She never!"

"Yep. Decked him."

"*And* he stayed decked. For some considerable time!"

They each sipped their coffee, smiling in remembrance of the historic blow. Beatrice mused.

"You know how wet Ma's been lately, Rach? Well when she laid into that little pipsqueak last night, it was as if she'd suddenly broken out, come alive again. I don't know, she seemed to be liberated somehow. She sort of dusted her hands and stood up straight and looked around as if she was ready to tackle anyone who bothered her ever again. I was so proud of her. Everyone was. It was a great moment in history when Ma KO'd little Charlie."

"Wish I'd been there. Hey, just a minute. Correct me if I'm wrong, but surely Ma's the one with the black eye."

"Oh that. That's nothing. As he went down one of his stupid cameras swung up and hit her. No one noticed at the time, everyone was busy cheering about George, and they gave a few cheers to Ma as well I can tell you. That newspaper should get a more tactful reporter, I reckon. The job's too dangerous for little Scoop."

"Did they take him in the ambulance as well?" — hoping not, George was entitled to sole use of the town ambulance at least.

"Not likely. Someone dragged him out of the way until he came to. Then I think Uncle Angelo chucked him into the back of his truck and gave him a lift back home. That Uncle Angelo, he's a character! Anyway, I better go back to Mamma. See you."

He caressed Beatrice's slender neck, and kissed her on the forehead. Rachel smoothed down her hair. Tried to smooth down her hair. Failed.

When he had gone, Rachel emptied her cup of coffee down the sink. "I hearby solemnly promise my body that I shall not drink more than two cups of coffee per twenty-four hours, from this day forward. I'm beginning to twitch." She came back to the table and faced Beatrice. "Hey listen, Bea. I want some answers to some pretty weird questions."

"I don't think I want to see a coffee cup for a few years either," Beatrice agreed, but in a tone that aimed to change the course of the conversation. "Listen, duck, Ma specially asked if one of us would go tell poor little Niffy or whatever his name is, and also that tall woman, that George has had the operation and can't have visitors yet. Only the family."

"Whiffy, his name's Whiffy," Rachel sounded, and was, defensive of old Whiffy. If he hadn't told them about the hideaway they might never have found George. "And it's Miss Follett."

"Whiffy, yes. They found him at the hospital this morning, well it was about lunchtime actually. He'd been there ever since they brought George in, and one of the wardsmen found him hiding in a linen cupboard. Lucky he wasn't suffocated, if they'd tossed more sheets on top of him he might have been. Anyway, he hadn't had any food, so they fed him and sent him off home. But Ma thinks it's only fair to let him know. And I said I would, but Rach, I'm so tired. Do be a duck and go instead. Please.''

Next time, I swear I won't give in to you, Beatrice!
"Okay. Give us a loan of your new jacket then."

The Walkers' house was closer, so she called there first, and Miss Follett was out. Helping at the Craft Centre so that Caroline could take time off to be at the hospital, Mrs Walker said. She had taken Bede with her, and his mother tried to give the impression that Bede, from the vast store of loving kindness he possessed, had offered to go so that he could help too. She failed to fool Rachel. Kind Mrs Walker was delighted to hear the news, and straight away went to the telephone to relay it to the Craft Centre, then she offered coffee.

"No thanks, Mrs Walker, but I wouldn't mind just sitting down for a minute. It's been a heavy couple of days."

It was alarmingly easy to deceive Mrs Walker, and Rachel felt bad about pretending to seem more tired than she actually was. With a rotten son like Bede, Mrs Walker had more than enough people taking advantage of her good nature. But she was delighted to serve, and brought cushions to stuff behind Rachel, and a hassock to put her feet on, so that it seemed cruel not to settle in for a while. The only trouble was that Mrs Walker was more inclined to talk than to answer questions.

But several anecdotes about her schooldays with Miss Follett gave Rachel an opening. A narrow, but useable one.

"Funny, isn't it," she murmured. "I mean, you going to

school with Miss Follett, and your husband going to school with Caroline."

"What do you mean, dear? How is that funny?"

Blimey. Do cooperate a BIT!

"Well, I mean, it's funny that Caroline went to school here, and I thought she was new to town. When she came here. About four months ago."

And raced off with my father.

Suddenly Mrs Walker's eyes became much shrewder than they had been, and Rachel felt a sudden sympathy for the evil Bede. It seemed that all mothers were the same: capable of seeing through brick walls. Eyeballs in their elbows!

"Well, dear, I think it's fairly common knowledge, I wouldn't be telling any secrets, breaking any confidences, if I told you that Caroline went to school here. She was born here, out of town, and they all went to the local school, your father, my husband Tom, Caroline. They were all friends when they were young. But Caroline, well Caroline went away, when she was twenty, and lived in Europe for a long time. My husband says that everyone thought she would come back after a while. But she stayed on and on."

"Why did she come back?"

And break up our happy home?

"You'd have to ask her that, dear. But Tommy says that when she came back, it was as if she'd never been away. I know that you must feel bitter, dear, her 'breaking up your happy home' as it were . . ."

Yikes! She can *see through brick walls!*

". . . but Caroline is a very special person. Very much like my friend Rose Follett. She makes everyone about her feel as if they are very special people too. She *pays attention*. Do you know what I mean?"

Rachel thought of the soothing presence of Miss Follett.

"Yes. I think I do. Well why did she leave?"

"There was a fire. A terrible fire. Her home was burned to the ground, and she just had to go away."

An image of a pile of blackened stones and three gaunt chimneys nudged at Rachel's memory.

"Her name is Caroline Summers. She lived at Summering," she whispered.

And Mrs Walker nodded.

16

So Caroline Summers and Mac Huntley had been friends when they were at school. Then when she was twenty Caroline went away, and stayed away for over twenty years.

Rachel felt that she needed time to work a few things out. A century might do it, if she had no interruptions. But an interruption occurred straight away. Mr Walker came home from the shop, fondly kissed his wife and gave Rachel a friendly nuzzle as he passed her on his way to what was obviously his personal armchair. Mrs Walker trotted off to fetch him a glass of sherry, and he unfolded the afternoon newspaper he'd brought with him. But Rachel was determined to get some answers. The news of the world would have to wait.

"Mr Walker," she began, in what she hoped was a suitably ingratiating tone. "I've got a problem here and I need your help. Please."

The dear man lowered his paper, folded it carefully in half and placed it on the floor beside his chair. He pushed his funny little half-moon reading-glasses right down to the tip of his nose and peered benevolently over them.

"Yo," he said, trying to sound much taller and a regular

man of the world. But his smile was too sweet for it to work.

And his nature was too generous to refuse to answer Rachel's questions, so he slowly sipped his sherry, and told her as much as he knew about her father and Caroline.

"We were all friends at school, but they were special, even as little kids. Always together. Wherever Caroline was, there was young Macintosh. Not that he trailed behind, you understand, don't get the impression that he worshipped the ground she walked on, silly nonsense like that. Thank you, my angel." The last bit was addressed to his wife as she topped up his sherry glass and Rachel got the distinct impression that some degree of silly nonsense like that certainly did apply in the Walker household.

"No, it was just that Caroline and Macintosh went together like, well, like hydrogen and chloride." He raised his bushy eyebrows, waiting for the laugh, and Rachel obliged, although if it had been her father making a tepid chemistry joke like that she would have had to kick him in the shin for it.

"Sounds funny, hearing Pa called Macintosh," she mused.

"Oh it was always Macintosh while his father was alive. A very stern chap was Huntley Senior. Poor Mac had a pretty tough childhood you know, being forced into such a rigid mould. That's why Caroline was so good for him, I guess. She encouraged him to be Mac, instead of Macintosh. Anyway, as they grew up we all just took it for granted that they'd marry. You know what it's like in these country towns." He sipped at his sherry, and looked down hungrily at his newspaper, but Rachel was implacable.

"So why didn't they? Go on, Mr Walker. I think I really need to know this, and I can't ask Ma, or Pa, or Caroline. Well, I suppose I could, but it's not easy you know, asking your parents stuff like this."

"Hmm, so our young Bede keeps telling us. We just can't communicate on his level, whatever that is, but he manages to imply that it's a lot higher than *our* level! Well, young lady, no one but they know why." Mr Walker nodded at his memories. "But I think there would have been a spot of difficulty there with Huntley Senior. Fond as he was of Caroline, he knew, I think, that if Mac married her she would help him slip away from his family's control. And incidentally, your father has a very highly developed sense of duty, young Rachel. He could have run off anywhere in the world with Caroline when she came back, but he chose to stay here. And I think it was so that he could keep an eye on you, his family. I'd like you to think about that, my dear."

I'll think about it later. Go on!

"But in those days it was the firm that his father wanted him to marry, the business that all the old Macintosh B. Huntleys had built up. Caroline might have shown him that he had a choice you see. Anyway, one Saturday night, the two of them were at the pictures in town here. I remember it so well, we were all there you see. Funny thing you know, it was *The Maltese Falcon*, and it's on again now. Had coffee together at the Blue Moon Café in the main street, we usually did that. And then Mac drove Caroline home. To Summering."

He stopped, and stared forlornly ahead of him for a moment, then he shook his head, took off his glasses, and wiped his eyes with his handkerchief.

"They saw the flames from the Bindah turn-off. The place went up like a torch and no one was there to help. So far out of town you see. Seems a faulty gas cylinder blew up, something like that. Nothing they could do."

"What about her parents? Didn't they even phone the fire brigade?"

"Mrs Summers suffered badly from arthritis, had

trouble even walking, let alone hurrying up out of bed and rushing out of the house. No, they didn't phone the fire brigade. Her husband was trying to carry her out of danger, the experts decided, and they were both asphyxiated by the smoke. They found their bodies, later. Together."

"Poor Caroline."

"She blamed herself, as people tend to do. If she hadn't chosen that night to go to the movies, if only she'd not stayed those few extra minutes in town, enjoying herself while her parents were dying, that sort of thing. It seemed that she even turned against your father."

"She was allocating the blame," Rachel nodded wisely, recalling Joe's words. "You think it helps at the time, but it doesn't really."

"Understandable reaction though." Mr Walker smiled his own understanding. "It's hard to bear alone, that sort of grief. Now look, dear, I mustn't keep you any longer. The thing is that Caroline had to go away, because she simply could no longer bear to be happy. To continue to plan a life with Mac seemed to her an abomination, I suppose, an affront to the memory of her parents. So she went away to Europe. We thought it was for a couple of months, but the time stretched out, and your father, I guess, was badly hurt. Then your mother came to live here, and . . ."

He shrugged. Rachel shrugged too, and stood up. She was sorry that she had no words that could properly express her gratitude to Mr Walker. She looked down at him, and saw for a moment not the plump, balding, bespectacled little pharmacist that she was used to, but the "verray parfit gentil knight" that his wife had been fortunate enough to see and recognise.

Mrs Walker had been in the kitchen while her husband and Rachel had their talk, and when Rachel went out there to say goodbye she had a container of food all ready in a string bag.

"Take this home with you, dear," she said. "You must all see that you eat well. It's important. So you make sure that they all have some of this. Right?"

Rachel took the food, and slung the handles of the bag over the handlebars of her bicycle. Then she went back into the kitchen, walked past Mrs Walker into the sitting room and across to the balding chemist, cocooned at last in his newspaper. She leaned over and kissed him on the forehead.

"Thank you," she said.

Then she went back to the kitchen where his wife was waiting to get on with preparations for their own meal, leaned down and kissed her too.

"Thank you," she said, and left them to their happy life together.

Whiffy was sitting in the driver's seat of the old car-wreck that stood in his front yard. There was no upholstery of course, so he sat on a slab of rusted metal, and picked with his chewed-down fingernails at the even thicker rust that encrusted the bent steering wheel. He merged well with the old car, being so dirty himself, and did not raise his head as Rachel approached. She propped the bike against the rear mudguard and climbed in beside him. Whiffy still did not move, but scratched with deadly concentration at his target. Rachel put out a hand and lifted his chin. Down his grimy face two trails of cleanness ran to drip off his chin. He sniffed.

"He's dead, inny? You come to tell me Georgie's dead."

"Hey, Whiffy, of course he's not dead. A doctor flew

up from Sydney this morning, a surgeon, and they operated on George and the operation was a success." She put her arm around the skinny little frame and recognised, with a pang of grief, a familiar form, the cherished shape of her brother.

"You know what, Whiffy? You're very much like George. You two could almost be brothers."

"Well we are, aren't we? Took a blood vow coupla years ago. He *rerly* gunna be awright, ya reckon?"

Much as she longed to, she could not promise him that. So she told him that there was a good chance, and he rubbed his face hard on his sleeve and nodded.

"Wasn't worried. Knew he'd be awright. Ole Georgie."

"Well it's pretty serious. I mean there's fractures and cuts and bruises and stuff, but the main problem is severe head injuries. That's why they got the surgeon up to operate on him. There's a possibility that George might have some brain damage, Whiff. He's in a sort of coma thing now and they don't know how long it'll be before he comes out of it."

If he comes out of it.

Whiffy had dropped his hands from the steering wheel, and he was very still.

"Hey, he's pretty healthy, you know. Just like you. He's really wiry, George is. The doctor says there's a good chance, and the family wants you to come and see him soon. Let you know when, eh Whiffy?"

"Sure. He'll be awright. Ole Georgie. We're tough, him and me."

So she gave him another hug and left him.

As she turned out of his gateway she looked back to wave. He was driving the car now, not picking at the rust. He was steering like a racing driver, with determination and purpose. And it came to Rachel's mind that he might be heading towards his gran, to help in her crusade against the landlords.

She hoped he was.

17

"I'm not at all the sort of woman who goes around beating people up! At least I never was. Until now."

"Well I must say, Janet, when you did decide to take up boxing you made a very good fist of it. That young reporter chappie didn't stand a chance."

Caroline interrupted. "Oh, Mac, do you mind! Made a good *fist* of it! That's a bit lightweight, isn't it?"

"I thought it was a knockout myself."

Ho hum. Why can't I ever do puns like Pa can. Hey!

"Listen you two, don't make a welter of it! How's that, eh?"

Her mother, enthralled by her new fame as a pugilist, and not inclined to play word games with them, spoke louder. "But the funny thing is, you know, that I felt so much better afterwards. I was quite wickedly thrilled when that offensive little boy went down. And let me tell you, if he'd had the audacity to stand up again, I would have knocked him down a second time."

Rachel patted her mother's hand, "Attagirl, Ma. Old Scoop had it coming to him, I reckon. How's your eye?"

The eye now exhibited a palette of colours that would

have delighted Miss Follett, but her mother ignored Rachel's enquiry and went on.

"Yes, I did feel better afterwards, and I still feel better. I know reporters have jobs to do, but there are limits."

"His father was always very pushy, wasn't he, Mac?" It seemed that here was another old school acquaintance of Caroline.

"He was, and believe me, Janet, if you hadn't clobbered the little beggar I would have. In fact, I was all ready to sock him one. You only beat me to it by a whisker."

Caroline and Janet smiled at each other across the bed, and Rachel realised that some sort of truce had been arrived at. It seemed to her that both his women knew Mac Huntley extremely well.

George lay between them, unrecognisable, all bandages and tubes and monitors, so that it was hard to find a spot to touch, for fear of dislodging something vital. Rachel desperately wanted to touch him. It seemed to her that strength could be shared, a will to keep living could be sent along her fingers into his body, if only she could touch him. She quietly eased the taut coverlet out from under the foot of the mattress, and slid her hand between the sheets. She found his leg enclosed in some sort of thick stocking, and despaired. But it was warm, so she gently laid her fingers on his instep and silently told him over and over again how very important it was that he should stay alive. She closed her eyes to give more force to her message, and the other three thought she had gone to sleep.

"Adores George," her mother whispered to Caroline. Then she turned her head and carefully touched her son's arm with her hand. "We all adore George. Can you hear me, darling? Well all love you very much, so please come back soon."

But George did not move.

Caroline stood up to break the cruel spell.

"Almost time for Bill Jarvis to do his rounds, isn't it? Why don't you two lie in wait for him here, and Rachel and I could nip down and have a cup of coffee or something. How about it, Rachel?"

It *was* time for Dr Jarvis and his band of interns to come, so Rachel admitted she was awake, gave George a final pat and a promise to come again soon and lend him some of her strength. Then she meticulously rearranged the coverlet and followed Caroline out of the ward.

There was one spare table in the cafeteria; there always seemed to be a place available for Caroline when she wanted it. So they carried their trays to it and Rachel set out a carton of flavoured milk, a cheese and ham croissant that had looked fresh and tasty in the cabinet, and now showed signs of having had a hard and busy life, in and out of the warming oven all day most likely. She had also chosen a bun with jam in the middle and what had seemed to be fresh cream on top.

"I don't understand it," she said, "it all looks so good behind glass, doesn't it?"

"No it doesn't," said Caroline as she unloaded her bottle of mineral water and small packet of wholemeal biscuits. "That lot looked just as repellant behind glass as it does in real life. Do your stomach a favour and have one of my biscuits."

So Rachel took a biscuit and munched it slowly, wondering at the fact that her mother didn't seem to be thinking of Caroline as "that woman" any longer.

"You and Ma seem to be getting along okay."

Caroline shrugged. "We're in an emergency situation at the moment. Maybe when she's not so worried about George she'll go back to hating me. If she ever did hate me. I somehow don't see your mother as a dedicated hater though, do you? She seems too basically kind for that."

"Dunno."

How should I know if she's a hater? I thought my parents were a happily married couple. Until you came back to town.

She picked at a corner of the croissant and tasted it. "This isn't as bad as it looks. Want some?"

Caroline, who had dwelt in Arles, shuddered and shook her head. "I hope she doesn't. Go back to hating me."

"Why should it bother you. You've got Pa. You've won."

Caroline took a long slow sip of mineral water and put her glass down on the table. "I wasn't thinking of myself. I hope for her sake she doesn't hate me. I want her to be happy, and hating corrodes the soul. Remember that won't you, Rachel. If you hate then you're the one who suffers, not the person you're hating. If you really want to hurt someone be indifferent, have no interest in him, nor sympathy for him, and *that* really will hurt."

She suddenly laughed. "My goodness, I'm moody today, aren't I? And of course I mean 'her' as well as 'him'. Hatred is no more sexist than any other emotion I guess."

"We all are. Moody. I had a talk with Mr Walker, he said he knew you when you were at school." Suddenly she was afraid to go on, afraid to admit to her knowledge of Caroline and her father and the tragedy at Summering. She felt that she had intruded, and that Caroline's present mood was too intense for safety.

Caroline cleared a spot on the table for her elbows, and settled her chin on her hands. "Dear Tommy, he's a good man. Listen, Rachel. You want me to tell you about your father and me, don't you? Well I'll tell you. But remember this is *my* version of the story, so it might not be the true one. That's the trouble with stories like ours, you can never be sure what's true, because everyone's version is different, everyone's version is true only for the one who tells it."

"You don't have to tell me. Really you don't."

But Caroline seemed to be talking to herself, not Rachel.

"There has never been anything in my life that felt so right as just being with Mac. When we were children I never doubted that we should always be together. We weren't alike at all, yet I always knew how he would feel about things, what would make him laugh, or cry, or be angry. I always knew."

She paused and Rachel hoped that someone would bound up and demand their table, shout that the hospital was on fire, or spill a glass of water down Caroline's back. Anything would be welcome that would break the spell and stop Caroline from going on. But nothing came to interrupt, and the dreamy-eyed woman opposite her went on.

"We never talked about marriage, just took it for granted I guess. In our day we didn't rush into living together, it just didn't seem so urgent to show how adult we were, particularly in the country. But we would have married."

She pushed a crumb around the tabletop with her fingernail.

"And then there was the fire. Summering was my home, I was an only child, and I loved my parents. I was . . . it was a Saturday night, I was at the movies with Mac and the others. It was *The Maltese Falcon;* we stayed on to have coffee and by the time we arrived at Summering my mother and my father were both dead. He tried to save her, because he loved her, and they both died. I loved them both, and I wasn't there to help them when they needed me."

Her eyes focused again. "You know, Rachel, for a long time I hated myself because I hadn't been there. I felt that if I couldn't have saved them, then the least I should have done was to die with them. Crazy. And then my hatred turned to your father. I guess there's a limit to how much blame, guilt, one soul can accept. You want to hand some over to another person to bear for you. And I gave it to Mac. I couldn't stand to be with him, because I told myself it was his fault that I had come home too late."

Rachel saw a movement near the door. Joe had come into the room and was looking around.

"Why did you come back?" she said, willing Caroline to make her answer succinct and quick.

Caroline's finger found a puddle of mineral water where her glass had rested. She began to draw figures in it.

"Caroline. Why did you come back? You'd been gone about twenty years!"

Joe was three tables away.

Caroline stopped drawing and looked up again.

"You know, I don't think I really know. There was some legal stuff I had to do with Summering, but I could have had someone else do that. I somehow just *had* to come back, Rachel. I'm sorry it messed up so many people's lives. I just *had* to."

Joe was at the table now. Looking tired.

"Do us a favour, would you Rach? Get's a cup of coffee?"

Oh sure. Get's a cup of coffee! Welcome to the family, Joe.

18

Beatrice answered the doorbell, murmured for a moment, then came back into the kitchen. She stood behind her mother's chair, rolled her eyes and dropped her jaw in an incomprehensible signal to Rachel, and said,

"Ma. A gentleman to see you. Says he won't come in."

Janet bustled out of the room and Beatrice collapsed on to the chair she had vacated.

"You won't believe this!" she crowed. "It's Scoop! Charlie Sutcliff, Ace Reporter!"

They peered together around the doorway and saw their mother, feet braced belligerently, glaring at the young man through the screen door.

"Scared to come in in case she floors him again, I guess."

"Wow, I don't blame him. She certainly made a mess of his face, didn't she?"

"Well, Charles. What is it?"

"Ook, Issus Untley," the battered lips enunciated. He tried again, "Not prying, honestly! Came to apologise. Ask about George. I *am* sorry."

Mrs Huntley's body relaxed.

She was *ready to hit him again. On yer, Ma.*

125

Mrs Huntley opened the screen door and dragged the very reluctant youth inside.

"Coffee please, Rachel," she called.

Oh sure. Coffee Rachel! Coffee Rachel! The Universal Coffee Machine, that's me.

But Scoop refused coffee, said he couldn't stand the stuff and made the announcement so firmly that Rachel gave him a second look. Despite the realignment her mother had done to his mouth and nose, he wasn't the weasel-faced wimp that Rachel remembered from school. He was about her own height, with fair hair and a pale skin, but his eyes were bright and sympathetic. And peering, so that Rachel realised that spectacles had probably been shattered in the fracas of the previous night.

"Hi, Rachel," he mumbled. "Still interested in tap-dancing?"

"Well, yes." Rachel slowly put down the electric jug and gave him a *third* look. "How did you know about that?"

"Into it a bit myself. Used to see you at Miss Arrow's classes."

Rachel moved closer. "I never saw you there. You mean to tell me you're interested in . . . gee . . . I'm sorry about your poor face, Charlie."

Janet Huntley coughed politely, and quite unnecessarily Rachel thought.

"I apologise for striking you, Charles. It was an extreme reaction I admit. But you can be very irritating at times you know!"

"I know. Not suited for the job." (With his swollen mouth it sounded more like "No hooted hor ha hob".) "Resigned. Leaving Friday. How's George?"

So they all sat around the kitchen table and explained the situation regarding George, and Janet finally agreed to let Charlie do his final story for the newspaper on the problems the family was facing.

As he left, Charlie turned to Rachel, winked his one good eye and muttered,

"Be in touch."

What d'you mean "Be in touch?"? Who'll be in touch? You with me, or me with you? Dammit!

"He doesn't seem so bad," Janet mused as they watched him walk down the path. "Perhaps I shouldn't have hit him so hard."

Darn right you shouldn't have!

"No. You should have hit him harder," Beatrice butted in. "Look at him now. He's crazy."

Charlie was doing a passable buck and wing as he proceeded along the footpath, and Rachel gave him a fourth, and extremely favourable look. Then he turned the corner out of sight.

The local paper lobbed on the doorstep early next day. Mrs Huntley was already at the hospital and Beatrice was getting dressed to go to college, so Rachel brought it inside. The whole front page was given over to George. There was a copy of last year's school photograph, with a heavy black arrow pointed at George in the second row of his class, and a blow-up of George alone. All teeth and hair and eagerness.

The headlines shouted:

LOCAL BOY HERO SURVIVES CLIFF DRAMA!
MISSING THIRTY HOURS IN NEAR FREEZING
CONDITIONS!

Cliff! Drama! Near-freezing! Hero! Wow, George will be pleased!

The copy below gave details of what had to be done to help George to recover. As Janet had insisted, no requests for help were made, the article was set out as a straight news story, but no cliché had been omitted, nor any florid touch of journalese, and Beatrice cringed with embarrassment. Rachel herself suspected that Charlie would make a far better career tap-dancing than he had in newspaper reporting, but she carefully flattened out the creases and hoped the newsagent didn't run out of copies before she could get down there to buy some more.

The paper had come at 7.05a.m., and by 7.07a.m., the telephone had begun to ring. Fortunately the second caller was Mrs Walker, to tell Rachel that Miss Follett was on her way with notebook and pen and would field the phone calls until further notice. In a few minutes, and seven phone calls later, the Volkswagen pulled into the drive and Miss Follett took over while Beatrice and Rachel set off: Beatrice to her lecture and Rachel to the hospital.

By the time Rachel and her mother dashed home for lunch a full-scale campaign had been organised. While Miss Follett was still taking calls, Mr Walker's shop was now the centre of operations, with the glamorous Sandra in charge there. She had an enormous diary on the counter, the biggest the newsagent could supply. Each day had a page to itself, with spaces for each hour. As people telephoned Rose Follett to volunteer, she thanked them and suggested that they call in to the pharmacy to work out which days and hours they had to spare, and which friends they could rope in to help.

The diary was filling satisfactorily, and when Rachel called in on her way back to the hospital she found the irascible manager of the cinema leaning on the counter making plans with Sandra.

"Way I see it is I flash this ad on the screen just before

we let 'em out for innerval, and just after the main feature, before we open the doors and let 'em go."

"They" sounded like a cage full of lions and Rachel guessed that to him they were.

"Nothin' fancy, eh? I reckon like, 'Your local hero needs your help!' Coupla big exclamation marks there, see?" He wrote the words in the air as he spoke and Sandra bobbed her head and soundlessly uttered each one after him. Her head bobbed twice and vehemently as the exclamation marks were punched into place.

"No experience necessary."

"Nethethawy," mimed Sandra.

"Enrol at Walker's Pharmacy. No! Correct that!"

Sandra shook her head and frowned.

"Contact Sandra, at Walker's Pharmacy. I'm throwing inna free plug for this place there see? On telephone, exetera." The message being now spelled out, his hand flopped back on to the counter.

I do wish people'd get that right. It's etcetera, et, et, et, dammit.

"Etthetera," Sandra murmured and wrote the telephone number down on an old prescription form for the manager to take with him.

When he was outside the door Sandra said, "He'th gone. You can come out now, Damien," and out from behind the counter crept Whiffy Baker.

Rachel *thought* she'd noticed something.

"Him and me we don't get on too good," Whiffy explained. "Reckons I sometimes sneak into his stupid place without paying."

"And do you?"

"Sure. He's pretty dumb. You pick up a ticket stub someone throws away after the show, and you can get in at innerval long's you like, prattically. Hey, I'm tellin' Sandy here I gonna organise the kids at school for this here thing

129

for Georgie. So how many you need you reckon? Fifty? A hunnert? Two hunnert? Say what you want and leave it to me."

"Whiffy, there's only about thirty kids in your entire school!"

"Listen. You want a hunnert kids, you got 'em. Right? I get you a hunnert kids, however many you want. No problem."

"Well thanks, Whiff. Great. How about we start with, say, twelve? The doctor says four at a time for a start, two to exercise his legs and arms and the others to sort of chat, play music, whatever, to stimulate his thinking, see? So three lots of four, twelve, that'd be a great start."

"Twelve for starters. Ya got it, Rach." And Whiffy strode importantly out of the shop.

"Cute kid," said Sandra.

Cute? Is this Whiffy Baker we're talking about here?

Rachel watched the little boy move along the street, straight-backed and stiff-legged, a soldier going to war on behalf of what she was sure was the only friend he had in the entire school. *Nobody* would listen to Whiffy.

"Yeah, is kind of cute, in a weird sort of way I guess. Gee, Sandra, I hope he manages to get twelve kids to volunteer."

"He will." And Sandra went back to filling in her diary, pairing up partners and allocating timeslots.

"Did you see that article in the local rag, Sandra? Great, wasn't it?"

"Hmm, not bad." Sandra tapped a perfect nail on a perfect tooth as she juggled her bookings. "A tiny bit hyperbolic but, didn't you think? Typical journalethe. You know?"

Rachel reeled out of the shop. Things seemed to be changing in this town. Definitely not what they had seemed.

19

George's room at the hospital was not big enough, so Matron decided that a suitable job for the first batch of volunteer helpers would be to clear an appropriate area so that the fight for George's recovery might begin.

The battleground selected was an old storage room at the back of the hospital, connected to the main building by a covered walkway.

"I'm not having my other patients disturbed by your noise," Matron barked, "so the farther away the better."

The group she marched at the head of comprised Rachel, the local stock and station agent who had been a colonel in the army in his day; the centre-forward of the district football team, big, beefy, burly Toby Griffiths, and the president of the Red Cross, wife of the local Member of Parliament, Mrs Dorothy Worthing, who had been to finishing school in Europe in *her* day. Big guns, all of them (except Rachel of course, a slingshot among cannons). Matron herself was small and silver-haired, but she put an awful fear into every person in town. The fear that they might one day fall ill, and thence into her hands, kept them all in well-disciplined order.

They and the next group of helpers worked all afternoon

to clear and clean the room. Matron sent down a spare bed (because someone was to sleep by George every night), some straight-backed chairs (because one even *sat* to attention in her hospital), an electrician to fix lights and ample power points, and last of all George. He looked, to Rachel, completely lifeless, head still bandaged, pushed by a cheerful wardsman with a nurse running beside the bed with a stand of bottles and drips, and Janet following with his spare pyjamas, dressing-gown and slippers, all bought new to help make him feel dapper and cherished.

By the following day the room had taken on the appearance of having been occupied for some years by a large and boisterous family. The unvenerable Bede had lent his complete stereo set of radio, record-player, and cassette deck. Joe's cousin Ricco brought in four large boxes labelled, HITS OF THE SIXTIES; HITS OF THE SEVENTIES; HITS OF THE EIGHTIES; and ALL TIME HITS.

Charles Sutcliff trudged in with music too. The dance music from every film Fred Astaire ever made.

Uncle Angelo brought his truck laden with Gina the athlete, her exercise equipment, four hyperactive cattle dogs (who were eager to stay), and boxes of fruit and plenty of wine to sustain the helpers. Rachel and Gina hid the wine in the clothes-locker so that Matron wouldn't find it, but Matron stumped in on an inspection tour five minutes later, flung wide the locker door, glared at the skulking group of bottles on the floor, selected one, held it up to the light and said,

"Looks like a good drop, Angelo. I'll take this one, thank you. Mind you keep them coming."

Rachel pedalled quickly home and fetched her bag. She hooked the golden ball to the top of the stand the drips were suspended from, placed the books on the shelf by the bed, hung the jeans and sloppy joe on the back of a chair, and set the kaleidoscope on the windowsill directly opposite George's bed, so that when he woke from his terrifying coma it just might be the first thing he saw.

Then the real work began.

It would be another five days before her own friends came back from the ski-camp, so Rachel spent most of her time as fill-in for other groups, and as self-appointed overseer. The physiotherapist came in several times a day to demonstrate the simple exercises. Nurses came and took temperatures, measured blood pressure, changed drips and dressings. Matron invaded daily to straighten sheets and to glare at the manic activity, but neither she nor any of her patients ever complained of the noise of the day-long comings and goings.

And it *was* noisy. Loud music played, loud voices shouted instructions and encouragement, and loud thuds and bangings accompanied the exercises. All this seemed to make no difference at all to the patient, but volunteer duty at the hospital soon became the pivot of the town's social life.

One day Rachel sat by the window and watched while Whiffy and his contingent worked on George.

First of all Whiffy leaned his elbows on the high bed and put his face close to the bandaged head, his denim-clad bottom sticking out quite perkily. Everything about Whiffy was perky these days. He no longer sidled, he stalked. He no longer mumbled, he spoke, and he was speaking now.

"Hey, listen here to me now, Georgie. This here programme me and the lads worked out for you today? Now we got the musical soundtrack recording a *Casablanca*. How about that, eh? Courtesy a your friend and mine-a, the dreadful, the D-grade, the dodgy, a-Donald a-Ducker!"

The other three in the group joined in to chant the poor

cinema manager's titles, and to drum on walls and floor loudly with the flat of their hands and their feet.

"The music's in the capable hands a Dimity here."

Dimity? Yikes! You mean that's a girl?

"Rest of us'll do the exercising and the talking and the moving about and stuff, right? Right guys?"

It was right with the guys so the session began. Dimity set the music off at full blast.

"Now today we got a rilly brilliant cast a thousands. We got Mick here. You remember Mick, George? Owny captain a the whole entire primary school, that's all."

Mick received the round of applause that he obviously felt was his due.

"Supporting cast, yours truly and Johnno here. Remember old Johnno, used to pee onna floor alla time when we was in kindergarten there? Well, he doesn't do that no more."

Rachel *was* relieved to hear it, but Johnno gave the sadly resigned look and shrug of one who had once possessed a rare skill and through no fault of his own had somehow lost it.

"And last, and quite definitely least, the old Dimity there."

The old Dimity darted across, whammed a mighty punch to within a hairsbreadth of George's shoulder, and bellowed,

"Hi, Georgie, gooda see ya. Attaboy!" and went back to adjust her volumes. Louder.

Johnno, the phantom piddler, prowled around the room picking things up and putting them down, singing along with bits of the music and doing a little shadow-boxing while Whiffy and the revered captain of the primary school each took one of George's feet and began to move it in a circular motion as the physiotherapist had shown them.

"Hey, I gotta scenario here. Remember that one we saw about the American kid and the bike riders?"

George made no sign of having heard, but Mick had seen the movie.

"Yeah," he growled, "I see that one. Great stuff. There's this kid . . . you better tell it Whiff."

"Nah," Whiffy protested, knowing his place. "Nah, you go ahead, Mick. You tell 'em better'n me."

But Mick insisted, and Whiffy, the perkiness showing even more, recounted the story of the film while he and Mick exercised George's legs, already skinnier and paler than Rachel thought they should be.

"Well, there's this kid see, and he's mad on Italy, says *'Ciao,* Papa', stuff like that, drives his old man crazy. The old man don't care too much for Italians see. Even catches him shavin' his legs one day, one reason or another. And there's this Italian cycling team coming to town, and he's practising so's he can ride with 'em. Well, see, you're him, like, George, practising see? You're pedalling round town, yellin' out *'Ciao,* Papa', stuff like that, and waving at all the girls."

Here Johnno and Dimity each seized an arm and George did some rhythmic waving to passing girls.

"Anyway, it's got this pretty sad ending. Am I right there, Mick?"

"Yeah. Pretty sad," agreed Mick.

Rachel wanted to hear no sad endings, so she left them then, marvelling at little Whiffy being deferred to by the school captain, to say nothing of the once-famous Johnno and the fierce Dimity. He seemed almost odourless these days too. Or maybe her nose was adjusting.

She met Gina and Ricco outside in the covered hallway. Ricco with his crash-helmet under his arm and a lot of dust on his face. He was shorter than she remembered. But certainly cute.

Gina was another problem. Joe was sure the two of them would get on well, but Rachel doubted it. For one thing, Gina was so bouncy. Like a female Tigger. Right now she was making small jiggling movements on the balls of her feet and her coffee-brown eyes were never still. Even her hair frizzed in an electric kind of way.

"Hi, Rachel, we're on next, with a couple of guys from the brewery."

She sounded as if they were booked to go ten rounds with the other two, and as if she was looking forward to winning the bout.

Ricco grinned at Rachel.

Cute. Yeah. Really cute.

"She wear you out too, huh?" he asked. "Hyperactive I reckon. Needs treatment."

"Am not," Gina protested, bouncing higher. "It's having all you boys in the family. Girl's gotta keep up."

Rachel guessed there was some real truth there.

"Hey, Rachel," Ricco was suddenly serious. "Beatrice was looking for you. Says it's urgent."

"What's it about?"

"Search me. The wedding probably. She and Joe've been doing a lot of talking lately. Planning I guess. She said to tell you to wait for her at home."

20

There was a message on the kitchen table much more verbose than the cryptic ones her mother usually left. It said:

> Rachel, I MUST see you to talk about this wedding. Also, Ma says you're NOT to spend so much time in George's room. You're to get some EXERCISE and FRESH AIR. SO DO IT. And DO NOT return to the hospital until you have seen me. I MEAN THIS! Beatrice.

For the languid Beatrice to advocate exercise and fresh air was a bit much, and Rachel was tempted to sneak off just to spite old Bossy-Boots, but the thought of wedding plans was a strong enticement to stay. By way of exercise she arranged herself on the old sofa in the breakfast room, and for fresh air she gazed out of the window to the side garden.

A pleasant place for a wedding. Spring would be the ideal time, perhaps late September. The old cast-iron table set out under the big fig tree in the corner there, spread with one of her mother's hand-embroidered and crocheted cloths, coming almost to the ground. The cast-iron chairs too, of course, for signing the register, and a huge bowl of white roses on the table. The sunlight gentle and the entire lawn speckled with rose petals. George is there as best man and Rachel as bridesmaid lovingly slides his wheelchair across the lawn to the tree. But Joe will probably want a cousin as best man — Ricco most likely — so George is groomsman, on crutches, and managing very well.

Herself in a blue spriggy dress coming down to her ankles, blue court shoes with the highest and thinnest heels ever seen, and perhaps a hat. Definitely a hat, a wide straw with lots of fruit and flowers on it and even a few bees here and there. Make-up provided by Sandra of Walker's Pharmacy, with the assistance of Paola Deladro, herself stunning in emerald green. The mother of the bride in deep rosy-pink that suits her so well, and the bride of course in white, all tulle, satin, and lace.

Around the other side of the house an enormously long table is set up with white damask and sparkling silver and glassware, and loads of sumptuous food. Beatrice and Joe sit at the head of the table, and they all drink toasts in Uncle Angelo's wine, and there is fun and shouting and laughter and people leaving their places to dash up and tell jokes to other people farther along the table.

A lot of Italian cousins, all male and about her own age, or a bit older, cluster around her and laugh as she tells them how she first felt about Joe, and how she claimed to have a bad back to stop him swinging her off the floor.

"You mean like this?" one of them says, and swings her around so that her skirts fly out and she has to clutch at her hat. Charles, nipping about with his arsenal of cameras, takes a snap of her before her feet are back on the ground, and looks annoyed about something. But later he partners her as they begin dancing on the wide veranda when darkness comes and fairy lights glow in all the trees and shrubs in the garden. Bede, free of his plaster now, cuts in and they laugh together as they dance.

Every person there is happy and friendly, even the ones who stared in the street and gossiped when Pa ran off with

Caroline. And George, with just a tiny bandaid on his forehead, is laughing and running about and wrestling on the grass with one of the younger cousins.

The happiest, most beautiful wedding there has ever been.

"Beatrice, have you gone mad? You have, Bea, you've gone completely mad, you know that, don't you? How can you possibly go and wreck your life like this! Beatrice! Look at me, will you?"

Beatrice flounced from room to room and Rachel flounced after her, finally running her to earth in the bathroom.

"Hey, buzz off will you? Give a person some privacy. I told you, Rachel, I'm not going to discuss it."

"Expect me to stand by while you throw away the only chance of happiness you may ever have?"

"Rachel, do you realise that you are talking just like your friend Charlie Sutcliff writes! You'd better watch that, my girl. I told you, I am not going to marry Joe. I do not wish to talk about it. It is none of your business anyway, and would you please go away and leave me alone?"

She pushed Rachel out of the room and slammed the door. Rachel yelled through the keyhole,

"Why? Just tell me why then! Beatrice! I shan't tell a soul. Promise! I swear! Truly!"

But all she had in reply was a muffled,

"Oh go tapdance up a tree why don't you?"

It seemed that it might take a while to wear Beatrice down. So she wheeled her bicycle out of the storeroom and pedalled back to the hospital to check on George.

21

"I can't understand Beatrice you know, throwing away the chance of a lifetime there. Wedding all planned and she ups and changes her mind. She's gone mad."

Her mother tugged at the sleeve of the green garment she was still unravelling.

"What do you mean, 'all planned'? She certainly hasn't discussed it with me."

"I had a cardigan that colour once, didn't I?" Mac Huntley picked up the front and held it up to his chest.

"Yes, you did," said the born-again Janet. "You certainly did. I knitted it for you. But you haven't any more. I'm making it up for myself."

Her husband put the piece down and said, "Oh," with no inflection at all, just "Oh". Then he turned back to Rachel.

"I got the impression you weren't too keen on the idea of your sister getting married anyway. Don't I remember you mentioning a few problems they might have? Too young, different cultures, different religions, stuff like that?"

"But I hardly knew Joe then. He's great. I like him. Did she break it off or did he?"

"Don't know."

"It's none of our business."

Her parents spoke together.

"She'll tell you if she wants to, some day, maybe."

Thanks Pa. Maybe. Be the first time anyone ever tells me anything at all.

"Time to go, love. Thanks for the meal, Jan." He bent and kissed Janet on the top of her head.

"Make sure you get some sleep now," she said, sounding like old times, but not meaning a word of it. Whoever did the night shift with George was expected to stay resolutely awake and poised ready to dash about in all directions and alert the world should George so much as stir. "And don't you stay too late, Rachel. Rose Follett said she'd drive you home."

When she and her father arrived at George's domain Miss Follett and her team were just finishing up, and the atmosphere was far away from some of the daytime bashes that Rachel had witnessed.

Music, sedate and soothing, was flowing through the room, and there was a strong smell of the herbal unguents that Miss Follett used to massage George's limbs.

"I promised to pop in to see Mrs Deladro, dear, so you have a good long visit with dear George here, and I'll give a tap on the door later," she whispered. "That's the last of his exercises for the day. He's had enough exertion, poor sweet lamb."

Then she and her cohorts crept from the room.

Rachel looked down at George, still inert. She had a sudden rush of violent anger and wanted to dash across and shake him back to life.

Oh come on George, you little beast. Stop fooling around. You can move if you really want to. Move, dammit.

Then she turned on her father.

"He's not going to start waking up while you're here. You know that, don't you, Pa? If he'd wanted to see you he wouldn't have run away in the first place."

Then she slammed across to the cassette player and switched it off. The silence was bleak and lonely. She pressed the button again and the sweetness came back, but brought no peace with it. Then her father walked across the room, took her throbbing head in his hands and pressed it gently against his chest. As she cried there she felt the wetness of his own tears on the back of her neck.

After a while he removed a hand and groped for one of the boxes of tissues that were stationed on just about every horizontal surface in the room.

"Here," he muttered, handing the box to her and fumbling a few tissues out for himself. "Pull yourself together, girl. You know we're only allowed one dramatic scene per day in this family."

Rachel honked, then decided to take the bull by the horns.

"Family! Huh! We're not much of a family any more, are we, Pa. I mean, really."

Her father led her back to the bedside and settled her in one of the chairs, sat in the other chair across the bed, and took one of George's tiny pale hands in his. Rachel blew her nose one more time and curled her fingers around the other hand.

Then her father began.

"Rachel's had a very difficult time recently, George, and so that we can all be concerned for her, we'll tell you about it."

"Pa! He mustn't be distressed!" Rachel hissed.

"We want him to come back to life, don't we? You know that's why we have all these people doing all these things to you, don't you, George? To bring you back to life, because we all love you so much and we miss having you around to drive us all crazy, which is what you do so well. And being distressed and being concerned about people is part of life. I think you know that, too."

Suddenly wanting to be the one to tell him, Rachel said,

"Beatrice now says she's not going to marry Joe, and George I think she should, don't you? He's fun, and he's kind and he's mad about her."

George did not reply, but her father did.

"You think she should now, do you? Different story a week or so ago, wasn't it, Ducks? But never mind, maybe they will marry some day, maybe some day she'll tell you why they decided not to. Or maybe they'll each spend the rest of their lives wandering the earth, seeking the half of themselves they have lost."

It was a weird thing to say, and his voice drifted off into silence after he'd said it, and there was only the soft music in the room. Then it stopped at the end of a movement, and Rachel looked up at her father. He smiled at her.

"It's an old myth I read recently. You know, since I left that shop and took up reading — as well as the writing of course — I've learned more about myself, about living, about *everything* than I ever suspected there was to learn. You two have the chance to start early in life. So read!"

"I am! We do! Don't we, George? Pa! You used to carry on like a madman because of us always having our noses in books! What's this myth?"

I thound like Thandra!

"I was reading a book about Plato, and there was a myth told by Aristophanes at Plato's Symposium. He was talking about the power of love and he said that in the first place there were three genders, Male, Female, and Man-Woman, and the form of every creature was round, so that when they desired to go fast they rolled, at great speed. And did I mention that each creature had four arms and four legs and two faces?"

Rachel didn't know whether a laugh was required here or not. She guessed not.

"No, Pa, you didn't mention that. And it sounds a pretty stupid story to me. What you reckon, George?" She squeezed George's hand. There was no response.

"Well I'll tell you anyway. These people were feared by the Gods because of their valour and strength and their proud hearts. So Zeus decided to cut each creature in two. This made them weaker but of more use to the Gods since their numbers were doubled. And now all those halves wander through the world, seeking one another. Maybe that's what love is, longing for the half of ourselves we have lost. Sometimes we never do find our other half and we have to settle for less."

Like when you married Ma?

"But that can be a kind of happiness too, you know. Look at your mother and me."

Yes, let's look at Ma and you.

"Caroline tells me you know about the fire at Summering. Well, when that happened and she went away I was in despair. I spent hours in that little hut I'd built for her under our pepper tree when we were children, so angry I bellowed, so sad I wept, until your dear mother came to live here and took me in hand. Gave me a home and a precious family to cherish."

Suddenly Rachel knew why she had persisted in pedalling out to that grotty farmhouse, cleaning up the kitchen, making all those thousands of cups of coffee. It was because she loved him. Because she loved all of them.

She squeezed George's hand because she loved him most of all.

And for a moment there, she thought she felt his fingers stir in hers.

UQP YOUNG ADULT FICTION

The Other Side of the Family   *Maureen Pople*

Katharine Tucker, fifteen, is sent from England to her grandparents in Sydney to escape wartime bombing. Once there, she's sent to the bush, to the strange township and eccentric home of her legendary Grandma Tucker.

Pelican Creek   *Maureen Pople*

Two teenage girls, living in a century apart, are drawn together by a secret in Maureen Pople's absorbing new novel for young adults. Living with friends in rural New South Wales while her parents' marriage breaks up, Sally Matthews finds a mysterious relic from the area's romantic past.

The Sky Between the Trees   *James Preston*

Not a book about superheroes, but about a farm boy who fulfilled his ambition to become one of Australia's great axe-men. This is the stuff that Australian myths are made of.

Blue Days   *Donna Sharp*

Marie Lucas has more than her share of the blues: her father has just died; her mother is in shock; her friends are disappointing and her boyfriend . . . Teenage life is complicated but Marie takes control at last. *Shortlisted — Children's Book of the Year.*

McKenzie's Boots   *Michael Noonan*

Six feet four and only 15 years old — and he ran away to join the army! McKenzie and his boots went to fight the Japanese in New Guinea, finding adventure, courage and a true humanity beyond wartime propaganda. A brilliant new novel from the author of *The Patchwork Hero*.

A Season of Grannies   *James Grieve*

Of all the hair-brained schemes that Jacqui Barclay is involved with, the Rent-a-Granny enterprise is perhaps the craziest. And it leads to others, including a very peculiar relationship with Looch, the Spaghetti Eater. *Shortlisted — Guardian (UK) Children's Book of the Year Award.*

Summer Press   *Rosemary Dobson*

Twelve-year-old Angela Read is left to her own devices one summer in the ancient village of Hadlow, England. She knows no one, but soon the forthright Lily, the mysterious and tragic Sarah, and a scarey silent boy keep her busy, and entranced.

The Boys from Bondi   *Alan Collins*

The world of young Jacob and Solly Kaiser falls apart when they are orphaned and pitched into a Sydney children's home which is filled with refugee Jewish children from Hitler's Europe.

Lonely Summers   *Nora Dugon*

Nora Dugon's appealing first novel is the story of a teenage survivor, Kelly Ryan, who befriends an impulsive elderly woman. Together this unlikely pair face excitement and danger in an inner city neighbourhood.

The Heroic Life of Al Capsella   *Judith Clarke*

Nothing is more important to fourteen-year-old Al Capsella and his friends than being "normal". Yet despite his heroic efforts to conform, Al faces a crippling pair of obstacles: his mother and father. *Shortlisted — NSW Premier's Literary Awards.*

The Inheritors   *Jill Dobson*

Twenty-five years after a nuclear war, a community of survivors live on beneath a protective dome. Sixteen-year-old Claudia, a promising youth leader, begins to question her society's oppressive values and wonder about life outside the dome's security.

Long White Cloud   *James G. Porter*

The Long White Cloud that guided the ancient Maoris to their new land is not the only cloud hanging over Gil Cook's head. His family has moved to New Zealand, to live on a small farm. When Gil leaves home intent on returning to Australia, he meets with more difficulties than he bargained for.

The Boy on the Lake   *Judith Clarke*
Stories of the Supernatural

In this spinechilling collection of weird and spooky stories, nothing is as it first appears. Judith Clarke's unpredictable imagination creates a very human world — charged with the power of mystery and the supernatural.

The Great Secondhand Supper *Greg Bastian*

Acting on inside information about a proposed link road, Jason Washington and his family leave the city to open a restaurant in Gum Flats. When the road fails to appear, the Washingtons are threatened with disaster. Jason plans to save the day by writing a prize-winning story, "The Great Secondhand Supper", and shares his ambition with Angela Conti, his vivacious schoolmate.

Clare Street *Nora Dugon*

A sequel to *Lonely Summers:* Kelly Ryan's seventeenth year brings her first experience of love and her first taste of a settled existence within her inner-city neighbourhood.

Merryll of the Stones *Brian Caswell*

A splendid story of time travel and magic which begins in Sydney, when Megan discovers she is the sole survivor of a motor accident. She awakes strangely haunted by dreamlike memories. When she goes to live in Wales, these lead her into a mystic ancient world.